"Dave Rose has a true gift of sharing the love and grace of Jesus Christ to the world through the power of creativity, drama, and humor. In "A Tree For Zacchaeus" David perfectly blends his many talents and life experiences into six unique and inspirational stories. Dave may be a short man, like Zacchaeus was, but his personality, heart, and passion are larger than life.

Even though I may tower over Dave in height...I will always look up to him."

Brian Kleinschmidt

Brian Kleinschmidt has appeared in several Lifeway videos as well as being on "Team Yellow" on the 15th season of ABC's Amazing Race with his wife, Ericka Dunlap Miss America 2004.

A Tree For Zacchaeus

TALES OF FAITH, HOPE, AND MYSTERY

David Michael Rose

CROSSBOOKS
PUBLISHING

CrossBooks™
A Division of LifeWay
1663 Liberty Drive
Bloomington, IN 47403
www.crossbooks.com
Phone: 1-866-879-0502

First published by CrossBooks 05/14/10

ISBN: 978-1-6150-7202-6 (sc)
ISBN: 978-1-6150-7203-3 (hc)

Library of Congress Control Number: 2010905756

Printed in the United States of America
Bloomington, Indiana

This book is printed on acid-free paper.

To my beloved wife, Pattie, whose belief
in me has kept this dream alive.

To my children and grandchildren: follow the
dreams the Lord has put in your hearts.

To my parents for never giving up on me.

To my brother and sister and their families,
find your dream its not too late!

To Pastors Danny and Jillian Chambers for your
friendship and covering. I am truly blessed.

To My Lord and Savior, Jesus Christ, thank you for loving
me so much. Thank you for your patience with me and your
never-ending belief in my finding the gifts you placed in me.

Contents

Foreword

Have you ever wondered why Jesus often used parables when teaching life lessons? Stories have a way of unlocking the tightest sealed heart and leaving a deposit of hope in the most hopeless of situations. In your hand lies more than just bedtime stories, what you are holding has the potential to encourage, inspire and even transform lives. Through the cleverly penned pages of author David Michael Rose, the limitless possibilities of living beyond the mundane into a life of divine destiny will become more than just another cliché. A life of magnificence will become attainable when you arrive at the inevitable intersection of decision where who you are now, and who you are destined to be meet face to face. It is at this crossroads you will decide to continue on the same path of worry, anxiety and fear or embark on a journey of supernatural trust in a Loving God to lead you out of the ordinary into the extraordinary. David's creative interpretations throughout these six amazing stories will no doubt capture your heart and inspire you to believe for the impossible.

Danny Chambers, Lead Pastor Oasis Church
Jillian Chambers, Co Pastor Oasis Church
CCO Puridigm Entertainment

From The Author

This book is meant to be interactive with the reader. It is best read with the aid of a highlighter or pen to underline a sentence, a thought or a section that causes you to think.

At the end of each chapter is a blank page for notes. I encourage you to, as you read, write down thoughts that come to mind. Hopefully something I have written will be that extra spark you need to motivate you to take the next step towards your destiny.

Take time to examine your own experiences with the supernatural aspects of God.

They are all around us, happening every nano-second, if we just take the time to look, think and marvel. Then ask Him to show you how to become the person He dreams you to be.

David Michael Rose

A Tree for Zacchaeus

CHAPTER ONE

THE PARTY

It was now the middle of Max's ninth birthday party, and everybody who was anybody was there! Every year Max had a party, and the middle was always the same: all the children would gather in a big circle around Max's Pa. Pa was what Max called his grandfather.

Pa would always tell a birthday story. Pa was a great storyteller. In fact, everybody enjoyed this part of the birthday! It was tradition to sit in a circle and listen to Pa tell a story. Last year it was "Goldie Rocks and The Three Bad Guys!" The year before that it was "Golden Blocks and the Three Boars." This year was the best! This year was "Golden Socks and the Three Bats." Pa was an original!

He told them about how the Three Bats came back to their secret cave hideout to find Golden Socks asleep on a pile of secret plans to rid the world of peanut butter. His right eyebrow would arch as he told them what happened when Golden Socks had awakened. His eyes squinted as he told the kids how the bats had tied up Golden Socks. Pa's eyes danced and his voice went high as he got to the part where Golden Socks had to use his secret shoe laser to burn the ropes, set fire to the plans, and stop the Three Bats from their evil plan to remove the single most important food group in the world ... second only to birthday cake! Throughout the story the kids oohed and aahed and gasped!

"Who wants cake?" asked Ma. Ma was Max's grandmother, and next to Pa's stories, her cakes were the best part of the party. Last year she made a cake shaped like the secret headquarters of Max's favorite super hero, Captain Lettuce Head! The Fortress of Saladtude … complete with the captain's sidekick, Crouton. The year before it was Dwinky the Stinkbug's Garden of Smells, with a lifelike skunk scent that made quite an impression on everyone. (Daryl Hanratty's mom is still trying to get the smell out of her nose!) But this year … this year was the best: an exact model of a duplicate of a copy of an original tracing of a reasonable likeness of Max's favorite theme park, Burp World!!!! (After all, you are only nine once!)

In a cloud of dust and a blur of feet, hands, and mouths, the kids zoomed into the dining room, sat at the table oohing and aahing over the burbling, gurgling, squirming cake that Ma had set out. There was Burp World in all its glory: the Slime Slide, the Twisting Tummy, and everyone's favorite ride, the incredible, amazing, colossal BELCHATRON! It was by far the most beautiful sight the kids had ever seen! Nobody knew whether to jump on a ride or just eat it! Finally, they dug in with gusto!

With Burp World just a happy memory, except for the crumbs and the icing on everyone's face, it was time for the most important part of the day: the presents.

Presents. The very word brought dancing images of toys, games, and fun to the minds of Max's party guests! Who brought the coolest present? Who brought the most expensive? Who brought the dumbest? A supreme contest every year!

All the packages were on display on the coffee table: big bags with a rainbow of tissue paper erupting out of them, boxes wrapped in colored paper and tied up with ribbons and bows, each one of them a mystery waiting to be solved. Next to Christmas, birthdays were the single most important day of the year.

Max looked over the bags and boxes, picking them up, weighing them, shaking them, as if he could tell what was in each one without opening them. He wasn't trying to guess anything; he was looking for the most important present of all—the one from Ma and Pa.

Ma and Pa. Next to his parents, they were the two most important people in his life. Every year of his long life, they had given him the best presents of anyone. It was tradition to open theirs first so that the kids could ooh and ahh in wonder. Max's parents gave him everything he asked for each year, but Ma and Pa knew the secret stuff that no one else knew he wanted. A bike one year, a remote control car the next ... no one else could come close! He let the kids play with any present he got, except for the ones from Ma and Pa. Those were his and his alone.

In the center of all the gifts sat a small plain brown package. Written in marker on the top were the words, "Happy Birthday, Max, From Ma and Pa!" No card, no pretty paper, just plain. Max looked around. Surely this was a joke. The two most important people on the planet, the undisputed king and queen of birthdays ... and this is all they did this year? Cut up a grocery sack, wrap a crummy box, and write on it?

"Go ahead, Max; open Ma and Pa's gift first!" his mother said. They knew the tradition. They witnessed the oohs and aahs each year from the kids. Max was almost embarrassed to even show he had noticed the present, much less open it.

He slowly picked it up. He turned it over and over, hoping Ma and Pa would burst out and say "April Fools!" or something and pull out his real birthday present. He waited ... nothing. He pulled the paper off and let it fall to the floor. It was a box. He lifted the lid off the box. Maybe there was a note inside, instructions about where to find the super present that had been too big to wrap. Maybe it was cash ... a check ... anything but ...

Inside the box was a smaller, old wood box. He opened it to find two things: a seed from a sycamore tree centered on a piece of velvet, and below it, a small plaque that bore the word "Destiny." Max just stared at it in disbelief.

"What is it, Max?" someone asked.

"Let me see, Max!" someone else said.

Max didn't hear them. He was in too much shock! His face wore *the frown*. Not the *I'm not happy* frown or the *I'm mad* frown. This was *the frown*. His mother recognized it, his dad too. Across Max's face was the special frown that only came on very special occasions. It was the *this is the worst day in the world* frown.

"What's wrong, son?" his dad asked.

"Nothing, just nothing!" an unconvincing Max said. "Thanks Ma and Pa, it's …" His voice trailed off in a mumble. He looked at the present, and then he looked at all the faces of his friends. It was all too much. He threw down the package and ran off!

"Max, Max! Come back here! You have guests waiting for you to open the rest of the presents!" his mom yelled after him.

"Don't worry," said Pa. "I'll hunt him down and bring him back. Meantime, you and Ma entertain the kids."

CHAPTER TWO

THE TREE HOUSE

Pa followed after Max, who had by now run out of the house, through the fence in the back, and directly to the one place Pa knew he would be: the tree house.

A tall stately sycamore tree stood in the center of the yard. Its branches stretched out and made a shade that hugged the back of the house. Midway up in the center of its branches, Pa and Max had built a tree house. Max called it his fort. It wasn't much—just some two by fours and plywood—but it was anything Max could imagine it to be.

Pa called out to Max, but there was no answer. He looked up in the tree. Pa remembered the last time he was up in that tree. He had fallen and broken his arm. He wasn't too keen on climbing up, but Max needed to understand the significance of the gift he had been given by his grandparents. This was too important. This had to be done!

But this … wasn't going to be fun. He looked up at the tree again. He sighed. What had he gotten himself into?

"Max! Are you up there, boy?" There was no answer. "Alrighty then, Mr. Tree. You better not jump, sway, jiggle, or try to shake me off! Anything happens to me, and my wife will fire up the chainsaw and make toothpicks out of you!"

Pa climbed the steps they had nailed to the trunk of the tree and gave the secret knock on the trap door in the floor. Max had to open it up. After all, Pa had used the secret knock. That was the rule.

Climbing into the tree house, Pa looked around and saw Max staring out the window at the field behind Ma and Pa's house. He was sitting on his basketball.

"Nice view," Pa said. "Want to come down and open the rest of your presents? The kids are waiting."

"Don't want to! I'd rather stay up here *by myself* if you don't mind!" Max said, emphasizing *by myself.*

Pa pulled the box out of his pocket. He had picked it up and brought it along. "Guess you didn't like the present," he said. "I didn't like it much when my Pa gave it to me when I was your age. I ran away too, 'cept I didn't have a tree house as cool as this to go to. I just ran out to the barn and climbed up into the hayloft."

"You mean you gave me a *used* present?!" Max said in a half-mad, half-surprised voice.

"That present was given to me on my ninth birthday by my pa, young man. It isn't used, it's ... well, it's a part of the history of this family. It has a purpose!"

Max could tell that Pa was getting a little upset with him.

"What's so special about this old seed?" Max asked.

"Well I'll tell ya!" Pa exclaimed. "But you have to promise me one thing."

"What?" Max said reluctantly.

"You got to promise me that you'll listen quietly, without interrupting, and when I'm finished, you'll apologize to your guests."

"'Pologize for what?" Max exclaimed.

"Do you wanna hear this story or what?"

"Yes, Pa. I'm sorry," Max said quietly.

Pa cleared his throat. He always did that before he started on one of his good stories. So Max leaned forward, resting his cheeks on his hands, trying to act like he was listening.

"You heard tell of the story of Zacchaeus in Sunday school?" he asked.

"Everybody's heard that story! Don't tell me that you're gonna tell me about that again. What's that got to do with this dumb ol' seed?" Max asked.

"Well, Mr. Smarty Birthday Britches, if you don't want to hear ..."

"I'm sorry, Pa, please; I want to know about the story. Please tell me," Max pleaded.

"Well, this isn't just an ordinary seed. This is a seed from a sycamore tree, just like the one we're in right now. You see, my pa gave me this when I was nine. He made me promise that I would give it to my firstborn grandchild when he or she was nine."

"Why?" asked Max. "Is it magic? Does it turn into a beanstalk or something?" The possibility of a magic seed and the potential to prove to the Winslow twins that thunder really was giants bowling in the clouds made Max's head swim.

"That's what I asked him. My, you are a lot like I was when I was your age. Full of questions! No, this seed is said to have come from the very tree that Zaccaheus climbed up to see over the crowd."

"No way!" said Max.

"Yes way!" Pa replied back "But this isn't a story about Zacchaeus. It's about how the tree got there in the first place."

"What do you mean?" Max asked with a puzzled look on his face. Pa was real good at tellin' stories, but this didn't sound like one of his usual ones.

CHAPTER THREE

BIRDS OF A FEATHER

Pa cleared his throat. He always did that just before he was about to tell one of his better stories. Max rolled his eyes but listened just the same.

"Well, it all started a few thousand years ago. See, there was a flock of birds that lived in a grove of trees far away from here. They were the most beautiful birds ever seen. They had bright colored feathers and a crest that curled up. They were proud birds and were by far the prettiest of all the birds in the land. They were especially proud of their tiny delicate looking feet. That is what they considered their most attractive feature, little tiny feet on big bodies.

"Anyway, they were right pretty except for one: a little bird we'll call Timus. He wasn't like the other birds. He was smaller, plainer, and he had one feature that set him apart from the other birds in his flock."

"What was that, Pa?" asked Max.

"He had the biggest feet of any bird in the entire grove! Yes, sir! In fact, all the other birds called him Bigfoot! They made fun of him, laughed at him, and generally made his life pretty miserable. Think about it. How would you feel if all your friends made fun of the way you looked and wouldn't let you do anything with them?"

"Well, they wouldn't be my friends then, would they?" said Max. "I'd probably be pretty sad if it were me!"

"Exactly! That is how Timus felt. He had no friends, no family, and no purpose. All the other birds were busy doing what birds do. You know—making nests, finding food, and flying ... bird stuff. All of them were going about their lives with purpose, except Timus. His friends had made fun of him for so long , and had refused to let him do anything important, that, well ... let's just say that he was feeling pretty sorry for himself.

"One day," Pa went on, "Timus was sitting in a tree, all by himself, when an Angel of the Lord appeared next to him. At first Timus couldn't believe his eyes! An angel was sitting right next to him. Right there in the same tree!"

"Guess he'd never seen an angel before," observed Max.

"Oh, he had seen plenty of angels. Animals see them all the time. It's people who have trouble seeing them! They get so busy with work and who's got the biggest house, drives the biggest car, who did what to who on "Days of the Edge of our Lives" and on TV reality shows that ... anyway ... he was surprised because the angel was sitting next to *him*, Timus, the plain brown little bird with big feet!"

"Don't be afraid, little one," said the angel. "I have come with good news! You have been chosen by the Lord for a very important task!"

"I'm not askeered of you!" Timus said loudly. "What would the Lord want with a plain little ol' brown bird with too big of feet? Nobody else wants to have anything to do with me unless they want a good laugh!"

"The Lord has a purpose for all his creations. He wants you to deliver something for him."

Timus stared at the angel. No one had ever wanted him to do anything before. He didn't know what to do.

"What does the Lord want me to do?" he asked.

"Take that seed from this sycamore tree and fly west. When you get to the right spot ... drop it on the ground. That's all, just fly to the proper place and drop the seed."

Timus looked at where the angel had pointed. High up in the tree, higher than any of the birds had ever gone, was a seed, gleaming in the sunlight. He looked back at the angel.

"We aren't s'posed to go up that high. No one has ever done that!"

"Why not, Timus?" the angel asked.

"Well," Timus paused. "Because, um ..." His voice trailed off. No one had ever said why he couldn't go to the top of the tree. It was just understood that you just didn't go up there. Timus couldn't answer him. All he knew was that feeling of fear when you looked up to that place. He just didn't know what it was that made him feel afraid.

"Timus, don't be afraid. In order for you to do this, you have to go higher to get what you need in order to do what you have been destined to do."

"But …" Timus started to say, but as quickly as he had appeared, the angel disappeared. Now Timus was alone with this funny feeling in his heart. Someone had finally asked him to do something. Something that seemed important.

"Angel!" Timus cried out. "Come back. How will I know where the right spot is to drop this seed?"

That's when Timus felt the most amazing feeling in his heart, a warm, peaceful yet energized sensation welling up inside him.

"Follow your heart, Timus … follow your heart. For the Spirit of the Lord will guide you and you will know." It was the angel's voice, but the angel was nowhere to be seen. It was as if Timus was feeling the voice deep inside.

CHAPTER FOUR

A Deep Breath

Timus looked up to where the seed was hanging. It seemed to call to him from deep within his plain brown big-footed little body. He looked around at all the other birds, wondering if they had heard or seen any of what had just happened. He started to call out to them, but something inside told him that doing that would just be asking for trouble. He closed his eyes, and taking a deep breath, jumped off his branch and headed upward to the top of the tree, the place where the seed—the seed to his destiny—hung waiting for him.

"Look at Timus!" he heard the birds say.

"Timus, Timus, come back down here. Are you crazy? We are not supposed to go that high!"

All the birds started to call him. At first he could understand them, but as he got closer to the seed, it sounded more like a bunch of noise. By the time he reached the seed, the cries of the other birds faded away. All Timus could hear were the leaves rustling in the breeze. He looked around for some great creature to pounce on him.

Surely there was something up here that was the source of everyone's fears … but there was nothing; just the sun. He looked over the grove that he had called home all his life. The view was beautiful: the colors, the hills, and clouds. He had never seen such beauty in all his life. He looked down where the other birds were. They were so small and dull. At this height, he couldn't make out all the colors of their beautiful plumage. In fact, they were just dots in the trees; silent little dots.

He looked at the seed. This was his destiny. That feeling started welling up in his heart again. He reached out with his beak and snapped the seed from the branch.

Looking out over the grove, he took another deep breath, spread his wings, and flew off into the unknown.

"Pa! Now just a minute. How did he know where to go?" Max asked. Pa must be slipping to let a big detail like that escape him.

"Well, I guess he was following his heart. Just like the angel told him!" came the reply. "Now may I continue?" Max's interruptions were irritating Pa.

At first the seed was so heavy. Timus couldn't remember having carried a seed that big before. He was used to little seeds or leftover pieces of seeds from other birds. The weight of the seed started to pull him down. He was slowly losing altitude.

Suddenly, the seed slipped from his beak. He tried to catch it but it slipped away before he could grab it. The seed, heavy as it was, rocketed toward the earth. Timus quickly shot downward, angling his body and pulling his wings back to dive as fast as he could. He had to get the seed before it hit the ground and got lost among all the seeds that had fallen from the trees in the grove. He knew in his heart that if he lost this seed he would lose his destiny. He was going so fast that his eyes were watering from the air rushing past him. He couldn't see clearly enough to make out the seed.

Oh I'll never make it! Timus thought.

"Believe!" It was the angel's voice again. "Believe in yourself, you can do it! You are almost there!"

"I can't see the seed. It's going too fast! My eyes, the wind, it's too much … I can't!"

"Timus, if you want to go back to the other birds, back to the way they treated you, laughed at you, made you feel, then don't try. If you want to discover what it really means to live life, then do it! Reach for your future, for your dreams!"

Timus knew he couldn't go back now. The other birds would make even more fun of him than they had before. He had no choice but to try with all his might. He stretched out one of his big feet, the very feet that had made him the laughingstock of all the other birds. The very feet that had made him an outcast from his own flock.

"Got it!" he exclaimed. He had caught the seed with his right foot and pulled back up toward the sky. "That was close!"

The surprise dropping of the seed and then the effort to catch it before it was lost had used up all his strength. He looked for a place to land. Then it dawned on him. He was now carrying the seed with his feet. He couldn't land now if he wanted to. He had to keep flying until he found the place where he was supposed to put it.

"Angel! Angel! I need your help! I am tired and can't land!" Timus cried out. Then he felt as if the wind reached out and picked him up and carried him.

"Don't be afraid, little one … I have you. Rest on the wind and let me carry you to where you need to go."

The voice came from within Timus again. Only this time, he didn't recognize the voice as that of the angel. A refreshing, warm, and peaceful feeling flooded over him. He wasn't tired anymore. He glided on the wind, resting, but moving forward toward his goal. He let go of any doubt or fear that he couldn't do this. He knew in his heart that he was going to make it.

"Wait a minute! Hold up!" Max interrupted Pa. "If that wasn't the angel talking to him, who was it?"

Pa looked at Max and smiled. "Who do you think it was, son?"

Max scratched his head, looked out the window, and then looked back at Pa. He saw the smile dancing in Pa's eyes. It was as if he was sending the message to him without speaking. A warm feeling welled up in Max's heart. "God! It was God!" Max blurted out.

"Exactly *Max*actly!" Pa replied. "God doesn't give you a destiny or a purpose for you to do by yourself. He wants to help you. You just have to call out to him and each and every time he will answer. Not just when you are tired, not just when you don't know what to do, but even when you know what to do. You have to learn to talk to him. Count on him for every little thing along the way so that you know in your heart you are headed in the right direction."

"What happened next, Pa?" asked Max.

Pa continued the story.

CHAPTER FIVE

COUNT YOUR TAILFEATHERS

Timus had been flying for three days. Never once did he get tired. In fact, he was amazed at how light the seed he was carrying had become. The sun had come up and was washing over the countryside. There were trees and hills. Timus had never been out of his tree and now, here he was in the most beautiful countryside he had ever seen.

Down below was a little stream with several trees around it. It looked so inviting.

That must be the perfect spot! It looks so peaceful and there are other trees, and water. Plenty of everything a seed would need to grow, thought Timus.

He started to slow down and look for a place to land. He circled around, lower and lower, looking at the water. It was so inviting. After all, he had been flying for three days, and he was thirsty. He could almost hear the water calling out to him. "Timus, Timus, come here!" it seemed to say.

Just as he was about to land he saw a large cat hiding behind a bush. He quickly pulled up as the cat jumped from his hiding place to pounce on him. The seed became heavy again. He flapped his wings harder pulling up. He could feel the spray of the water as it splashed on the rocks in the stream. The cat reached out to swipe Timus out of the air. His claws stretched out, mouth open, ready for the meal he was about to feast on. Timus closed his eyes and made one last push. He cried out for help. A gust of wind lifted him just as the cat's claw barely brushed his tail feather. Timus soared upward, his heart pounding, lungs feeling like they were going to explode!

"Don't be afraid, little one. I am here. I have you. I will protect you!"

It was the same voice again. The same voice he had heard when he had gotten tired.

"Who are you?" Timus asked.

"I AM," said the voice.

It was then that Timus realized that it was the voice of the Lord, the creator of all birds and all living things. Again the peace washed over him as the wind carried him forward, away from the danger.

"Lord?" asked Timus.

"Yes, little one?"

"Was that you who came to me earlier when I was tired?" asked Timus.

"Yes, Timus. I am with you always."

"Why did you pick me to do this?"

Silence. The voice was gone. Timus looked around. Up ahead he saw a clearing next to a very well-worn path. Suddenly, a warm feeling welled up in his heart and his feet began to tingle. He looked down. He was over the clearing and next to the path was the angel. Timus circled around. The angel was pointing to a spot close to the path that men had made with their camels and wagons. Timus landed next to it, letting go of the seed that he had been carrying for three days, just before he touched the ground. The seed dropped, bounced, and rolled into a little hole next to the angel.

"Don't worry," Timus said, "I'll get it."

"No need, little one," the angel said. "This is the right spot. Didn't you feel it? Couldn't you tell?"

"You mean that warm tingling feeling I had? That was how I was supposed to know that this was the right spot? Is that all? What if you hadn't been here? What if ... did you know I almost got eaten by a cat? Where were you?"

The angel held up his hand to silence the burst of questions that exploded out of Timus. "You were never in any danger. Didn't the Lord come to you when you were tired? Didn't he come to you and rescue you from the cat that was lurking where you weren't supposed to be? Need I go on?"

Timus knew that the angel was right. Every step of the way, the Lord had been with Timus on his journey. Even when he was where he wasn't supposed to be, the Lord had rescued him and brought him to the right spot to plant the seed.

"What now?" asked Timus.

"It is time for you to go, little one. This part is done. Go, find a grove of trees and start a new life. Tell everyone about your journey. You will have a long life." The angel slowly began to fade.

"Wait, Angel, come back! What about the seed? What was all this about?" Timus cried out.

The angel continued to slowly fade, but as he did, he answered Timus. "You have done well in the Lord's sight. Go now to your reward of a long and prosperous life! Don't worry about the seed. You planted it. That was all you were meant to do. I will stay and guard it. You see ... by your obedience to the Lord, obeying his direction, and setting out to fulfill your destiny, you have now placed this seed where it can begin to grow toward its destiny. You have done well, little one. Now, go and be blessed." And with that, the angel finished fading, dissolving into thin air right before Timus's eyes.

Timus looked around. That puzzled feeling that had led to the burst of questions that he had blasted the angel with was now replaced with perfect peace. He rested in a tree nearby for a little while picked a direction that felt right, and flew off into the clouds.

CHAPTER SIX

Wait, There's Got to be More!!

"Wait! That's it? He flies off into the clouds? What about the seed? What about the tree? What about Zacchaeus? That can't be all there is to it!" Max exploded.

"Max, Pa, where are you? We have guests waiting to open presents!" It was Ma coming out to see what was keeping them.

"Be there in a minute, Mother." Pa called out. "Just having some man talk with my grandson!"

Ma smiled to herself. She had heard the story at least a hundred times in the thirty-seven years she had been married to Pa. She knew just how important this was not only to Max, but also to Pa. It was the completion of Pa's destiny. She walked back to the house, knowing that it would be all right. She closed the screen door behind her.

"Who wants to help me make a cake?" she said to the waiting kids.

"Pa ... Pa, you have got to finish the story. You can't just leave me hanging here. I have to know what happened. I want to know how this seed is my destiny. You promised!"

Pa sighed deeply. "Alrighty then, Max ... you are right. That is not the end of the story. However, before I go on, you have to make me a solemn vow!"

Max looked at Pa and then looked at the seed in the box. The little gold plaque seemed to glow, and the word *destiny* seemed to leap off the plaque and jump right into Max's eyes.

"What's a vow?" Max asked.

Pa cleared his throat. "A vow—a solemn vow—is the most important kind of promise you can make. You're not supposed to make promises you don't plan to keep, but if you make and break a solemn vow ..."

Max blinked. Pa had him. Max thought about all the presents Ma and Pa had given him over the years. The bikes, the skateboards, even the cakes Ma had made him every year. He couldn't remember Pa ever asking him to make a "solemn vow" before. This was serious. This was important. This was the only way Max was gonna hear the rest of the story. It was possibly the greatest story he had heard Pa tell him his whole life. What could Pa possibly ask him to promise that would be so hard? He cleared his throat, opened his mouth, and nothing came out. *Solemn vow* echoed in his mind.

"Now, before you say yes … you think about something, young man. Your ma and I, we love you with all our hearts. We do a lot of things for you because we love you so much. We don't give you presents because we have to … we give you presents because we want to bless you. We want you to know how special we think you are. The way you acted today, in front of your guests, in front of your mom and dad, well, that said you didn't love us unless we give you some high–dollar, fancy–shmancy, need–a-degree-from–Harvard-just-to-put–it-together kind of gift. This gift, this means more to me than anything I have ever owned. My pa gave it to me and made me promise what I am about to make you promise. I may let you get by with a lot of stuff in life, 'cause I'm a grandpa and that's my job, but if you make this promise, I will hold you to it for the rest of my life!"

Max gulped. The rest of Pa's life was a long time. After all, Ma and Pa were gonna live forever!

"Pa, before I make this solemn vow, I want you to know something. I don't just love you and Ma when you give me presents! I love you because I know you love me. I wouldn't want to do or say anything that would hurt you, honest! I'm sorry."

There was a twinkle in Pa's eyes. He took a deep breath and motioned for Max to come over to him. He gave him a big hug.

"I know, Max. I just wanted to see if you knew. You see, a lot of times we say or do things that hurt the people we love without even realizing it. We just expect them to do something. It's called taking them for granted. That's something no one likes to feel. Being taken for granted." He paused. He then looked deep into Max's eyes. They were tearing up in the corners. Pa told himself he wasn't going to cry but he could feel his own eyes watering a little. He was just about to tell Max the vow he wanted him to make when he felt a warm tingling sensation come over him. He had only felt that once before, when his Pa made him make the same vow Max was going to have to make.

CHAPTER SEVEN

THE PROMISE

"Now Max, you have to promise me, give me your word, that you will keep this seed until your grandson turns nine. You can tell the story all you want, but you got to promise that you will not let the seed leave your possession. It's important that you understand that I'm talking about a long, long, long, long time. Not just a day, not just a month, not even just past Christmas, I am talking about when you grow up and get old like your ma and me. Now that is a long time and that is why this is a solemn vow."

Max took a deep breath, let it out, and in his best grownup sounding voice, said, "Pa, I promise to keep and protect this seed. To not let anything happen to it, until my grandson turns nine and I can give it to him and tell him the story." He then held out his hand to shake on it.

Pa smiled. He reached out, took Max's hand, and shook it.

As he stood there looking at his grandson take his first step towards manhood, Max spoke again. "Pa?" he asked.

"Yes, Max? What is it, son?"

"Okay, I know I made this solemn vow, and I know that one day, I will have a grandson I will give this seed to ... but ..." His voice trailed off.

"What, son? You can ask me anything."

Max cleared his throat. "Does this mean ..."

"What, son? Speak up!"

"Does this mean I have to kiss a girl? 'Cause if it does, then, I don't know ... I mean ..."

Pa stood up, smiled, and laughed. "No, son, you won't have to kiss anyone if you don't want to. However, I promise you, when you get old enough, you'll want to! Believe me .... you will want to!"

Max sighed an instant sigh of relief. "That's good. Jimmy Winestacher kissed a girl and said that to this day, chocolate tastes like Brussels sprouts!"

"I don't think that will happen to you, Max, my boy! I think when the time comes ... well ... how about we finish the story! Now, where was I? Oh yeah ..."

CHAPTER EIGHT

THE REST OF THE STORY

The angel stood guard over the little seed Timus had delivered. Whether it rained or snowed, or got blisteringly hot in the sun, the angel did not move. If a wagon pulled by horses or a caravan of camels came by, the angel would reveal his presence to the approaching animals. Somehow they could sense the importance of that spot and would simply step around it. As time went on, a tiny green shoot pushed its way up through the ground. Year after year, the angel stood his ground, making sure that neither man nor beast trampled the young sapling.

After many, many years, at last, the little seed grew into a giant Sycamore tree. Its branches spread out, hugging the little clearing and path with its shade, making an inviting place to sit, rest, talk, climb, or sleep.

One day a small plain brown little bird flew up and landed in one of the branches.

"Timus! He came back!" cried Max.

" No, sorry, Max, too many years had gone by. Timus grew old and died. He was very happy and had many, many children and grandchildren," Pa said.

"Then who else could it be?" Max asked.

"It was the great, great, great, great, great, great, great, great, great—" Pa paused and took a deep breath. "—great, great-grandson of Timus."

The little bird looked around. It was then that the angel appeared sitting on a branch next to him.

"Hello, little one … you made it."

"Who are you and how do you know who I am?" the little bird asked.

"I knew your great, great, great, great ... I knew Timus. I am the angel the Lord sent to show him his destiny. You are also Timus," said the angel.

"Yes, I am Timus's descendant. I have heard of his story from my parents. They said it has been passed down through the years and that he was the greatest amongst all the birds of our flock," the little bird said proudly. "Now I have come to find the truth about this story and to see this special spot I have heard so much about. I just landed here to rest before I go on. My parents said that I would know it in my heart when I reached the spot. They said I should follow my heart like my namesake did. I don't know if I believe this story or not. I want to know for myself if it's true."

"And what does your heart tell you, little one?"

"That it's tired, hungry, and thirsty."

"Rest here, little one. For you have found the spot. You see ... this tree we are sitting in is the very tree that grew from the seed your ancestor planted here so many, many, many years ago. It has grown tall and strong and is now ready to meet its destiny."

The tree shook slightly and startled the little bird.

"Earthquake! Earthquake!" Timus cried as the tree continued to shake.

"No, little one. Its not an earthquake. Look down. See that little man climbing up into the tree?" The angel pointed down to a man, the littlest man Timus had ever seen, climbing up into the tree, which was now surrounded by a crowd of people.

"What's he doing climbing up into this tree? Does he think he's a monkey? Does he think he's a bird? What's he going to do?" asked Timus.

The angel was silent. His attention was focused on the man who was walking up the path toward the group of people who had gathered under the tree. The tree stood tall, stretching out its branches to block out the sun. It could feel a tingling in its roots as the man approached. People lined the path, and they surrounded him as he got closer to the tree. Timus could hear children laughing and saw them dancing around the man as he smiled at them and laughed back.

"His name is Zacchaeus. He is the reason the Lord asked your ancestor so many years ago to bring the seed here. He is the reason I was assigned to guard the seed to keep it safe from being trampled so that it would grow into what it is now. This tree will enable Zacchaeus to catch the attention of that man as he walks past," the angel answered as he watched intently with anticipation as the destinies of Timus's great, great, great *and so on* grandfather, and the tree, and Zacchaeus were about to merge into one.

Timus looked at the little man in the tree, the man walking up the path, the people below, and then back at the angel.

He was about to ask who the man coming up the path was when the angel said, "The man walking up the path is Jesus. He is the son of the Most High God. This tree, planted by the first Timus, will help Zacchaeus meet Jesus, who will then change Zacchaeus's life forever. You see, Zacchaeus was a small tiny man who thought that by becoming a tax collector and cheating people out of their hard-earned money, he would become big in the eyes of others."

"Zacchaeus, Zacchaeus … you come down. I wish to come to your house and eat with you!" It was Jesus calling out to the little man up in the tree. Timus watched as the little man jumped down, almost falling out of the tree to go meet this man, Jesus.

As the two men walked off toward the house of Zacchaeus, the angel turned to Timus. "You see, little one, your great, great, great, great, great, great, great, great, great (sigh), great, great grandfather, Timus, was the very reason this tree was here. Had he chosen not to listen to me, the Lord's messenger, and chose instead to stay where he was, neither of us, certainly, none of this, would have happened. I would not be here, the tree would not be here, and you would not exist."

Timus looked into the eyes of the angel. He could see the truth in those eyes. He couldn't deny the warm feeling welling up in his heart or the tingling feeling in his big feet.

"Angel, do you think the Lord would mind if I stayed here and made this tree my home?"

"Follow your heart, little one … follow your heart." And the angel disappeared.

Timus stayed and lived a long, happy, fulfilled life knowing that because his namesake had followed his heart, Timus was able to witness the destiny of his ancestor come full circle back to him. It was a good feeling that Timus never forgot to celebrate, nor did he ever forget to thank God daily for everything.

"Well, Max, what do you think? Not such a dumb present after all, is it?" Pa said as he finished the story. "Max? Max!" he called out.

Max was no longer in the tree house. As soon as Pa had finished, Max scooped up the little box containing the sycamore seed and scurried down the tree, heading toward the house.

"Max ... Max ... where are you going?"

Max stopped in his tracks. He turned around, revealing *the smile.* This was reserved for those special moments, those times he was the proudest or happiest.

"Gotta hurry, Pa! I have a destiny to keep! I have to tell the story to my friends. This is the coolest present ever!" Max yelled back excitedly.

As Max ran back to tell his friends the story of the seed, Pa leaned back in the tree house. The sun was starting to turn those colors it does when it slowly begins to melt into the western horizon. He had completed the destiny his grandfather had given him. He felt a warm feeling welling up in his heart.

"Thank you, Lord. Thank you for destinies!"

The sun continued a slow, languid dissolve into the horizon. Just outside the window where Pa sat watching, a small plain brown bird with big feet perched watching the same sunset.

Thank you, Lord. Thank you for destinies! the little bird thought. He turned to see Pa there. He hopped over from the branch to the window and chirped.

Pa looked over and saw him. "Timus?" a bewildered Pa said.

The little bird turned as if to fly off into the sunset.

To this day, to hear Pa tell it, that little bird winked at him before he flew away.

NOTES

NOTES

Run

The punches were consistent. Each one measured, calculated, concise. The pain was immeasurable. The whole time I kept hearing him say, "Who's your daddy? Who's your daddy?" Mike Tyson was using me as his personal punching bag. I was hanging upside down, helpless as the relentless punishment continued. That's when I woke up.

My son, James, three and a half, was standing beside the bed, punching me while screaming "Wake up, Daddy! Wake up, Daddy!" The last punch landed squarely in the nose, causing me to leap out of bed, scare James, and me to trip and land on the floor of our bedroom.

"What happened?" Kate nonchalantly called as she came in the room. "Come to Mommy, James."

"What about me? I'm the one who's been mortally wounded," I said while rubbing my throbbing rudolphian proboscis.

"I'm sure you'll survive. There is coffee when you are ready. I have to get James ready to take over to Mom's, and then Jan and I are going shopping."

"Shopping, Jan, Mom ... got it!" I said as I slowly stood up to face the morning.

I stumbled into the bathroom and mumbled incoherently as I began my Saturday morning routine. "Yes sir!" I said to myself. "What'll it be? The usual shave and comb over?"

"Naw, I think I'll go au naturel this morning. Thanks anyway!" My reflection stared back at me. I kept waiting for one of those

"Twilight Zone" moments where the reflection talks back to you, makes some derogatory comment of your general state, and then offers some sounds-too-good-to-be-true solution. Never happened while I was looking; mirror must be defective.

I grabbed my robe and headed for the porch. The paper would be just arriving and with the house to myself, I looked forward to the deck out back, coffee, and the news of the world.

Kate kissed me goodbye, and James slobbered a jelly toast kiss on the side of my face. "We'll be out most of the day honey. You gonna be okay?"

"Yeah, I got the yard and the lawnmower to keep me company!" I quipped as she and James loaded up to head off on their adventures.

Kate was beautiful. She lost all that weight she'd gained from the baby almost immediately. She had gotten on some South Carb diet beach or something like that and had stuck with it. She and her sister, Jan, walked everyday. She was amazing.

I looked down; my toes were just barely showing under my somewhat prosperous waistline. Ahh, donuts! I looked up to see the new addition to the neighborhood run by and wave. He was, I don't know, maybe in his late sixties, early seventies. Thin, bald, gray, and sweaty. He moved in three or four doors down, but you know how it is. When we were kids, everybody knew everybody by name in the neighborhood. People would come out on their lawns, or porches, talk, share recipes … the good old days. Nowadays, you were lucky if you even saw someone. This guy was so new; he didn't know the rules—move in and stay invisible. He will learn.

I went back inside with my paper, got my coffee and donuts, and headed to the deck to relax. Watching that guy run had worn me out. The rest of the day was spent sitting on my lawnmower riding in circles and making everything look perfect. For three years in a row, my yard had won first place in the Homeowners' Association annual beautification contest. Round and Round in circles … the Stepford Yard.

Not much else happened for the rest of the weekend, really. Time just sort of oozed past unnoticed, and suddenly it was Monday.

I went out to get the paper, this time with donut in hand. There he was, the new guy, gray, bald, sweaty, running, waving, and smiling. I shook my head and went back inside. *Get a life*, I thought.

The weeks to follow just sort of ran into each other, like most of my thoughts. Every morning there was the new guy running and waving at me as I stood on the porch in all my perfection.

It was about six or seven weeks after this whole run-wave relationship had started that I noticed that when I looked down, I could no longer see my feet. At first I panicked. I raised my leg just to make sure all the toes and everything were attached. They were. They were just covered by my abundance. That is when *he* ran by and waved. I shrank down in embarrassment. Here is this guy, twenty-some years older than me, thin as a rail, with more energy than I had in my entire body. I went back into the house, into the bathroom, and looked in the mirror.

"Self," I said, "you need to get out there and do something, now. Step away from the donut!" I went into my closet, found my tennis shoes, and put on some shorts and the cleanest T-shirt I could find.

"Kate, I'm going for a walk. I'll be back in twenty minutes!" I yelled.

There was no answer. I called out again. Usually James would yell back. Silence.

I walked into the kitchen and saw the note on the fridge.

"Gone to Jan's. Have James. Will call. Kate."

"Gone to Jan's?" I said aloud. She had been doing stuff like that a lot lately. Going to her sister's, or her mom's. We were rarely home together any more it seemed. Roommates—we had become roommates with the only connection being our son, James.

I sighed the "oh well" sigh, turned, and headed out the door. The old man had long past gone by the time I got out. Just as well. I was not up to a Laurel and Hardy moment.

I got about a block and a half when the lungs gave out. I was sweaty, panting, and my knees were yelling at me to stop, turn around, and go home. This was not a good sign.

I was gonna have to do something about this. I stared straight ahead. I could hear the theme from *Rocky* playing in my head. I took a deep breath, and then with all the determination I could muster, turned and walked back to the house, back to sanity, back to … donuts and coffee.

The next day, I woke up early for some reason. I just could not sleep. I got up … 6:30 in the AM. This was not good! It was too early. I went to the porch for the paper. There was that guy … running … waving … mocking me! "I'm older than you, but I could run circles around you and your donut!" That is what his running and waving was really saying.

"Oh yeah, well I'll show you! You old goat!"

He looked at me funny and then ran on. It was then that I realized I had taken leave of my senses and had had my half of that conversation out loud.

"Alrighty then. Have a nice day!" I said loud enough for him to hear. I looked around to see if any of my neighbors had heard that. I grabbed the paper and went back inside.

I grabbed my walking shoes, shorts, and cleanest T-shirt, and got dressed. This time I was determined to get farther than a block and a half! Have you ever seen those scary movies where the person is staring down a long hall, and suddenly it seems to get longer and farther away than you thought? All the while, whatever evil was chasing the person seemed to be bearing down on him, taunting him. "You'll never escape me!!! Ha ha ha ha ha!!!!"

The road I was walking on gradually rose upward to this impossible hill. It was the kind of hill that kids on bikes and skateboards dream about; it was an alpine ski jump.

I do not remember if he passed me or I just saw him up ahead, but the sweaty old man was taking that hill like it was nothing. His stride never slowed down. In fact, it looked as if he was picking up speed as he neared the crest. I rubbed my eyes and looked again as I could have sworn I saw him turn and stick his thumbs in his ears, wave his fingers, and stick his tongue out at me before turning and popping over the hill, his bald head disappearing like the sun on the horizon.

It was getting late. I had to get back home and get ready for work, but something inside said that if I didn't at least make it to the top of that hill, I would never be able to live with myself. I pushed on. I tried to remember all the themes from the Rocky series, any James Bond movie—something to move me further toward my goal. In what seemed like forever, I finally made it to the top, turned, and loped down the hill toward home, coffee, and my old friend and constant companion, the donut.

Work is usually uneventful unless Curtis is feeling his oats. I work for a small accounting firm. Curtis is the office clown. Maybe he is more like the office's *evil* clown. He has a penchant for acidic witlessness. Today, Curtis was in rare form! I usually try to ignore Curtis. Today though, I took the bait.

"Hey, Kupa, looks like you're in the running!" his New England accent butchering the pronunciation of my name, Cooper.

"The running for what, Curtis?" I asked.

"They're thinking about finding a replacement for the Goodyear Blimp!"

"Curtis, I will have you know that I have taken up walking lately, and I am getting in excellent condition!"

"Oh, did they open a new Crunchy Crème donut shop on your block?"

That was Curtis. It didn't matter to the upper echelon that the rest of us in the office carried his load while he joked and quipped and ripped up everyone and everything with his "humor." They liked to send Curtis out to entertain the clients. The clients liked him, and that was all that mattered. The rest of the day was spent avoiding Curtis. I had gotten good at that lately. I made it home without incident. Home ... sanctuary.

"Honey," Kate called, "I found these tennis shoes out on the bedroom floor. They look like they've been ... used."

"I took them for a walk this morning. We had such a good time that I'm thinking about doing it again tomorrow!"

She looked at the shoes, and then back at me; she was confused. Her husband, walking ... it was almost too much. I smiled, blinked my innocent little eyelashes at her, and changed into my usual jeans and T-shirt at-home attire. Kate came over with the tennis shoes, kissed me on the forehead, hugged me and said, "Next time you two are out, remember to brush off before you come in." I gulped. Kate hadn't kissed me on the forehead in along time. She hadn't kissed me, period. I made a mental note to make sure I got up and walked again in the morning.

The morning came early. I hate it when it does that. Kate and I had been up talking, actually carrying on a conversation until 11:30 that night. The kiddo was in his usual nocturnal coma, and we actually lost track of time. So when the alarm went off at 5:30, I started my usual groan, flailed for the snooze button, and stopped. Wait, I won't snooze! You snooze, you loose! I'm no loser! I'm a ... (*Yes, yes* the voices in my head said in unison, *say it! Say it*!) ... I ... am ... a ... *walker*!

I jumped out of bed, tripped, and rolled into the entertainment center, startling Kate for a second. Then I got myself into the bathroom and actually shaved my face and brushed my teeth before getting dressed for my walk. I grabbed my shoes and headed for the kitchen, surprising myself by walking right past the donuts and over to a banana that was out alone in the "nobody ever eats this but it looks nice in the kitchen" fruit bowl. I peeled it and took a bite. This banana was the best tasting, sweetest, mushiest banana I had ever eaten. (At least I think I've eaten bananas before.) It had several dark spots on the skin, which usually means that we haven't been to the store buying fruit in a few days and it's time to throw it out; still, that is when they are at their sweetest. I licked my fingers, got my bearings, and headed for the front door. Now, it was early enough in the morning that I was going to get a good twenty-minute head-start on the old new guy. What a shock it would be for him to see me ahead of him by a good lead!

The shock was on me. There he was, running by and waving. It was like he had been watching me and knew I was up early. Little doodads crept up my neck. Was this my *Twilight Zone* moment? I looked around. No Rod Serling, no "doo doo do doo, doo doo do doo" music playing. I was in the middle of the block, so there *was* a signpost up ahead, but it just said *stop*. I shrugged and decided that early or not, by gum I was gonna walk no matter who did or didn't see me!

I stretched my calves, my knees, my thighs, and my neck. I yawned (thus getting my arms and back into the stretch). I then started out on my walk. Since I was early, and there was no one else except *him* out, I decided to walk in the middle of the road. How refreshing! The concrete sidewalk was a haven, and now I was truly walking "on the edge"! The road had a strange energy to it. It crept up my legs, and my arms and back twitched, like a switch had been turned on. Next thing I knew, I was doing a light jog. And then, after a few feet, I was picking up the pace, and by a full block and a half I was running. It was amazing, beautiful, and scary at the same time. Here I was on the road, before six AM, running. Too bad Curtis wasn't here to see this! I stretched out my arms like wings, took in a deep breath, and coughed up one lung and then the other. Maybe it was a good thing Curtis wasn't here to see that. "Lungs, expand, I command you to expand!" I shouted in my head.

"Feet, take us back to bed!" They seemed to yell back. I was determined. If that old geezer could do this every morning, so could I! *So could I!*

I continued to run for a couple more blocks, thinking that if I could keep up this pace for another block or two, I could turn around and possibly meet my arch nemesis halfway.

What a shock it would be to him to see me coming back while he just getting started. I smirked a little and then almost stopped in my tracks. There he was, cresting over the hill, coming back toward me. I felt humiliated. I thought I was ahead of him, that I had gotten the better of him. I thought that possibly for once, I was going to do something that would shock him back to wherever he came from and this would be the end of my running. Oh the humanity of it all! I was devastated!

Maybe it was just my imagination, but I swear there was an evil glimmer in his eyes as he smiled and ran by me. It was almost as if he were telepathically saying *I am better than you and I always will be*! I felt something snap inside and I started running harder, faster, up, up, up the hill! For a full thirty seconds I gasped, gulped, and sputtered to the top of the hill. Once I was at the top, I turned to gloat … and he was gone. In the time it had taken me to force my way to the top of the hill, he had somehow managed to make it back to his house and disappear.

My triumphant taking of the hill was now a moot point. I fought the urge to merge with donuts at home and instead continued my jog. I began to appreciate the effort, and I realized that for the first time in a long time … I was having fun. In the weeks to follow, I continued to push myself. I was now running a full two miles every day. I was skipping donuts. In fact, I shocked Kate when I told her to no longer buy donuts. I told her that I wanted fruit in the mornings instead. She had that strange "what have you done with my husband?" look on her face, but she agreed.

The weight was dropping off and I looked closer to my old college days, when Kate and I first met. She even commented on the fact that I was going to have to buy some new clothes. She began asking me when I was coming to bed. Usually she just put the kid to bed and then herself … but lately … she wanted to snuggle, she wanted to talk … she wanted me!

Work was getting better. Having more energy, I took on more work. I found and fixed problems. My bosses were noticing me more and more. The coup de gras came when one of them stopped by for advice. Curtis came over and was launching into one of his "post-lunch soliloquies." The boss looked at me, looked at him, and point blank asked him, "I'm sorry, what do we pay you to do?" Priceless! The look on Curtis's face said it all! Not only did the boss shut down the show, he asked Curtis to come to his office in fifteen minutes with every account file he had been working on. Seems there were too many errors this quarter and Curtis's clients weren't happy with the level of service they were paying for and not getting!

The next day, I got up at 5:00 AM wide-awake and ready to run. I could not explain it, but something told me that today was going to be my best day ever! Not only was I up, I was not concerned about whether "you know who" was up and out. In fact, he didn't even cross my mind as I hit the street and ran my two miles in my best time ever. I even ran an additional mile, it felt so good.

As I was finishing I noticed I had not seen my competition that morning. As I got closer to the house, I noticed the "for sale" sign in his yard. That was strange. Seems like he had just moved here and now he was leaving. I shrugged, went inside, showered, and headed to the office.

The day started slow but soon picked up, and I was up to my eyeballs in tax returns when the big boss came to my desk.

"Cooper, there have been some discussions amongst management as to your role here in this office ..." His voice trailed off. I braced myself. This is the how you start a conversation that ends badly for the non-boss person side of things. I looked at him. He seemed larger than I remembered. I sputtered a little but I couldn't seem to get any words to come out. My brain froze and my antiperspirant seemed to scream it couldn't take anymore and left.

"As you may or may not know, Cooper, we had to let Curtis go this morning. He just wasn't working out. This leaves a big gap in the workforce that we want you to fill. Now, before you say anything, let me just add that with the added work, you will be given a substantial raise, and we are watching you. We are looking for candidates for a new vice president and you, Cooper, are in the running!"

I was stunned! I didn't know what to say. I just stared at my boss and blinked.

"Why don't you take the rest of the afternoon off? You have been working hard and you deserve it. Come Monday morning we will discuss your future with the firm in much greater detail."

I stopped by the florist and bought two dozen of the most beautiful roses I could find. I called Kate's sister, Jan, and asked if she could discretely weasel James away from Kate for the night. I went home, showered, changed, and took Kate out to eat at her favorite restaurant. I told her about what had happened at work, about the possible promotion, how everything seemed to be going my way.

She put her arms around me ... and then stopped. She stepped back, looked at me, stepped forward, and put her arms around me again. This time she squeezed. It wasn't just one of those "I'm proud of you" hugs; no, this was more of an "I don't remember the last time I could put my arms all the way around you, but it sure feels good!" kind of hugs. I hugged back and realized I had forgotten just how good she felt in my arms. That old spark was back, and I leaned her back and planted the biggest kiss I could muster right on her lips. She kissed me right back. I got the check, and we rushed home. It was a blur of clothes, arms, and mouths, but we made love like we had never made love before. I laid back on the pillow and passed out with her in my arms. This was the best day ever!

The next morning, I woke up early and decided to run. Maybe I would see the old man, and I could tell him thank you for unknowingly being my inspiration! The morning air was crisp and my lungs were singing its praises as I crested the hill. No sign of my muse, but I was having the best run of my life.

That afternoon I noticed a woman in the yard of the old man. I walked over. Maybe he was home, and I could shake his hand.

"Hi, my name is Cooper. My wife, Kate, and our son, James, live across the street and two houses down. I'm embarrassed to say this, but I have been meaning to come over and introduce myself for a while. I see your husband out running every morning."

At first she just stared at me as if in disbelief. Then disbelief turned to anger. "Is this your idea of a joke?"

"I don't understand. I mean ... I'm sorry for taking so long to introduce myself. Now you're moving and I feel like a complete idiot for not doing this sooner!"

"First of all, you couldn't have seen my father running every morning. He has been dead for more than six months! Cancer. He used to run. After he was diagnosed he took up running. He said he had always wanted to run a marathon and was going to do it before he died. Well, he didn't make it, and I think it is so uncaring of you to come over here and ..." Her voice trailed off in tears. I just stood there my mouth open, jaw touching the ground ... the entire time I had been running after this old man ... he had been dead.

"Ma'am, I am so sorry, I had no idea. When did he pass?"

She seemed to regain her composure as she told me of his passing. He had gone out for a run six months ago, the day before he was to run the marathon. He came back and said he was going to lie down for a while. That was the end. Six months, that was when I first saw him and began my quest to catch him. She was here to sell the house, clean out his stuff, and move on with her life. She was his daughter.

I went back home in shock. Kate was awake and James was running through the house yelling, "I run like Daddy! I run like Daddy!" I told Kate the whole story about seeing this old guy running and how it irritated me so much I took up running. I explained how awful I felt that I had made him my enemy and how I vowed to best him without ever thinking about getting to know him or anything about his life.

Kate, being Kate, just looked me right in the eye and told me how much she loved me, how proud of me she was, not only for doing so well at work but for taking the initiative to run. She was proud of me for thinking about not only our marriage but our family and me as well. She was worried that she was going to be widowed at an early age because of the lifestyle I was or wasn't living. She was worried that James wasn't going to have a father. All of this was going on in her head, and I had no clue. The old man may not have gotten to run his marathon, but he accomplished one thing. He showed me how to live.

The next morning, when I got up to run, I ran with a purpose. I wasn't going to take any second of my life for granted anymore. From this day forward, I was going to live every second, appreciate everything and everyone, and most importantly, I was going to run a marathon … before I died.

Notes

NOTES

The Story

Dill stared at the blank screen. He had sat in the same position for more than an hour. Nothing. He had made this big deal about why he couldn't go with his wife, Donna, to a school parent-teacher meeting.

"No, honey, I can't go! I have to write. You know our future depends on my finishing these stories. No stories, no book; no book, no publishing; no publishing, no money. No money ..." He stopped there.

Donna looked at him in disbelief. For weeks he had lain around the house watching TV, surfing the Internet, doing everything except write. Now that she asked him to do something important the "muse" comes to him and he has to write?

She glared at him for a minute and then said a silent prayer. *Lord, give him the words tonight. Give him whatever he needs to do this, but make him do this!*

With her teeth clenched and her purse and keys in hand, she took their daughter and headed to the school.

Dill was alone. First thing he did was to go downstairs to the family room. His office was next to it. He got as far as the TV, and the remote control all but leaped into his hand, begging for its buttons to be pushed and stroked. He flipped through the channels, stopping at *The Wonderful World of Wrestling*. Klondike Karl and Little Jackie Ripper were going at it for the North American Wrestling heavyweight title. He had been waiting for this match for weeks. It was everything he had hoped it would be. Klondike was known for his dirty, underhanded methods and Little Jackie Ripper was known for his high-risk highflying maneuvers in the ring. Klondike had Jackie in the "Bear Trap," His favorite, most-painful submission hold, when the signal was suddenly lost.

"No! Not now!" he cried out in disgust. He went over to the window; it was storming outside, and with the wind, rain, thunder, and lightning, he had just about everything one would need for a satellite dish signal interruption!

"Well, now what, Dilly ol' boy?" he said to himself. "What, pray tell, are you gonna do now?"

He looked over at his office door. He cringed. He looked back at the snow on the TV screen … and then back at his office. He thought for a minute. If he couldn't write anything upstairs on his laptop, what made him think he would have any better luck in his office? Once again he looked at the TV in hopes the snow was gone and he would see who the new North American Wrestling heavyweight would be, but once again the blizzard of snow gave him no signal.

"Oh all right! I guess I'll actually write something!" he said angrily as he walked over to the office door. He pulled out his keys and unlocked it. As he walked in, the computer was playing a piano piece, soft, low, and worshipful. Dill kept music going twenty-four hours a day in his office; it was his way of maintaining an atmosphere of peace.

This used to be his pastor's office. He and Donna had bought the pastor's house a few months before. Donna was so excited about Dill getting into that office. After all, this was where the pastor had written so many of his great sermons and so many great songs. The tears from his prayers were soaked into the carpet. She just knew the anointing that had been poured into this office was going to pour itself into her husband. Oh, the songs and books and stories he would write! She believed in him so much and was so proud of him! She spoke about these things every day. She wanted her man to know how much she believed in him. If only he believed in himself, maybe, just maybe he could get something done.

Dill sat at the computer and stared at the screen. An hour later he was still staring, wondering what to write, or even if he could write. He had had a few bursts of inspiration when they first moved in, but there wasn't anything happening now. Dill had even taken to getting up at 4:00 in the morning to pray and study his Bible ... but that had turned into a pray-and-check-his-e-mail ritual. He seemed to have lost something, but he couldn't really put his finger on it.

Donna was going to be upset when she got home. He hadn't done anything! Squat! Nada! He was washed up before he even got a chance to get wet.

"What am I going to do?" he said out loud. He closed his eyes, rubbing them in a mixture of mental fatigue and frustration. He looked up at the screen one more time, hoping for a sudden burst of creativity, and there it was ... a sentence. No, more like ... a question.

"Why don't you ask me?"

That was all it said. Dill looked around the room. He was alone. He looked down at his hands; they were still attached. Someone had to have written that ... but it hadn't been him!

"Okay, this is getting to be a little too Stephen King-ish for me!" he said. "Who wrote that?" He laughed. He had finally lost it. He was talking to an empty room.

"I did."

Dill jumped out of his seat. There on the screen were two new words: I did.

He knew he was losing it now! There was no way he had written that. His hands weren't even near the keyboard.

"Who are you?" he typed. The cursor blinked off and on, throbbing as if it was about to burst from the screen.

"I AM."

Dill started to shake. His computer had just typed two more words right there while he was watching.

"Oh my sweet Lord, save me!" he screamed.

"I did ... when you were six. Remember?"

Dill remembered. He remembered the traveling preacher who had come to his daddy's church. He remembered that funny feeling in his heart when the preacher asked anyone who needed Jesus to come on down. That was the longest walk he had ever made in his six years of life. That preacher was so big and sweaty. He spit when he talked and he smelled funny, but the words he spoke went right into Dill's heart, and he knew at six that he needed Jesus.

Wow! he thought. *I haven't thought of that for years!*

"I know," was written across the screen.

"Wait a minute, what do you mean, 'I know'? What's that supposed to mean?" Dill stared as the words danced across the screen effortlessly.

"It means you haven't thought about our relationship in a while. It means that you have just been going through the motions ... but your heart hasn't been in it for a long time. You've become, dare I say, religious."

Dill began to sweat a cold, nervous, scary-movie kind of sweat. Something or someone had tapped into his computer and knew some very personal stuff about him.

"Who is this really?" Dill typed.

"I AM I AM I AM I AM I AM I AM I AM I AM I AM I AM I AM I AM." The words filled the screen, over and over, scrolling down several times as if filling pages and pages with these two powerful words. A quickening rose up in Dill's spirit. He knew that this was an uncommon supernatural visitation. It was exactly as his pastor had described happening to him many times when he would come down late at night to pray or work on a sermon. Now it was happening to Dill.

He shook, blinked, and began to type. "Why are you here?"

"I am always with you, Dill," was the reply on the screen. "I have been with you since before you were born. I was there with you when that car almost hit you when you were four. You had run out into the street chasing that ball. I picked you up and threw you out of the way."

Dill remembered. To this day his mom tells the story about how he had been in the front yard playing with his cousins. They had thrown the ball to Dill, but he was younger and slower so it hit the ground and rolled out into the street. Dill ran after it. He wanted to show his older cousins he could keep up. He saw nothing but the ball in front of him. He didn't see the car; he didn't even hear the horn. One second he was staring like a deer in the headlights, next thing he was on the other side of the street, the driver of the car screaming, asking if he was all right, his mom screaming about a miracle and his cousins staring in disbelief.

They had seen Dill, had seen the car tearing toward him, and they knew it was going to be messy but they couldn't look away. Right before their eyes, as if he had sprouted wings, Dill rose up over the oncoming car and landed safely on the grass on the other side of the road. It was as if he flew like an angel. Everyone had seen it! The driver threw out the whiskey bottle in the passenger seat, fell on his knees, and prayed to Jesus right then and there. Dill's mom was dancing her miracle jig as she practically smothered Dill in a hug so tight he could barely breathe. Yeah … Dill remembered.

"That was just the start, Dill. I was with you when you smoked your first cigarette. Do you remember getting sick?"

Dill nodded.

"Dill?"

Dill blinked and then looked at the screen again. "Oh," he typed, "I am sorry, I was remembering the incident with the car."

"It's all right, Dill. You were really too young to realize what had really happened. I don't want to get into a long good-ol'-days thing. I just wanted you to know I have always been with you and have never left your side. Even when you were where you weren't supposed to be or doing what you weren't supposed to be doing … I was there with you. Protecting you. I have too many great plans for you to let anything happen to you that would keep you from fulfilling your destiny."

"Why do you care so much for me?" Dill typed in response.

"You are my creation. I am the Creator. I have a special interest in you. I made you. I gave you your gifts and talents, the ones you have struggled with over the years. I have so much invested in you. Do you think I am gonna let that investment go to waste?"

Dill stared back at the screen. Tears welled in his eyes. For the first time in years he felt that love. It was so pure, so strong so … right. He couldn't help but cry. No man, no matter how big or tough, how smart or rich or poor could keep from crying in the presence of God.

"Why have you come to me now, Lord?" Dill typed.

"I'm answering a prayer."

"What prayer? I don't remember praying for anything...."

"You are not the only one who prays in this house. Donna has asked me to give you a story."

"Donna? What? What do you mean? What story?"

"This story, your story, my story ... our conversation is your story."

"You mean this is my story, the one I'm supposed to write? C'mon ... nobody in their right mind would read this! It's too ... too ..."

"UNREAL?" scrolled across the screen.

"Yes!" Dill typed in response.

"Uncommon, supernatural, close encounters kind of thing? That kind of unreal?"

"Yes!" Dill typed. "No one would believe this ... I mean ... I'm not even sure I believe it and I'm the one talking to you. Typing, I mean."

"Dill, Dill, Dill! You need to stop right now and think about what you are saying! For someone with a gift for words, you sure aren't acting very gifted! Now, scroll back through what we've typed and read a little. Go on ... read it back to me, out LOUD!"

Dill shook his head. He couldn't believe what was happening. God was having a conversation with him via his computer. It was like he was using some Holy Ghost instant messaging service.

"I'm waiting, Dill! Read!" typed across the screen.

Dill obediently scrolled back through the pages he had typed during the last thirty minutes. He began to read out loud the conversation. A warm peaceful feeling came over him. There it was. His story: new, fresh ... something different.

"Okay, Lord, I get your point!" Dill typed. "This would, I mean *will* make a good story. It will be a good addition to my collection of short stories I am putting together. What should I call it?"

The cursor just pulsed. No words came across the screen.

"Lord?" Dill typed.

Nothing. Dill heard the garage door open up. Donna was home. He quickly titled it "The Story," hit save, and then hit print. The paper couldn't shoot out of the printer fast enough! He burst out of his office and leaped up the stairs.

"Donna, Donna, you're not gonna believe what just happened! It was so ... I mean ... I got my story.... You gotta read this!"

Donna hadn't seen Dill this excited about anything for years. She accepted the story as Dill took their daughter up to bed. She felt the tears well up as she read the first few sentences.

It was her prayer that this would happen, that Dill would hear from God and use this precious gift he had been given. She stopped, grabbed a box of tissues, and sat on the kitchen floor. The conversation unfolded in her mind as it did on the paper. She could even see Dill's expressions as he reacted to what God had typed to him.

Dill came back down the stairs after tucking in his little girl. He started into the kitchen looking for Donna. He stopped when her heard her voice.

"Thank you, Lord, for answering my prayer. Please let my husband know there are many, many more stories in him. That you are going to bring them out and that he will be published. O Lord, I give you all the praise ... all the glory."

Tears started down Dill's face. Not only had he been in the presence of God, now he knew he was in the presence of a godly woman. A woman who, despite all his faults as a man, as a husband, still loved and believed in him so much that she covered him in prayer. Dill fell to his knees. Somehow there were no words ... just tears of worship, praise, and thankfulness. Somehow Dill found the greatest gift a creative person could ever have: a conversation with the Creator.

NOTES

Notes

A Test of Faith

It was raining when Dan pulled into the church parking lot. The rain trickled down the front window on the passenger side where the seal had rotted through. He sat quietly, collecting his thoughts, waiting for the rain to let up. Thunder rolled across the sky and crashed into the dark clouds overhead. Dan didn't notice it as there was a louder thunder crashing inside his heart. Jack was leaving.

Jack had been the pastor of the tiny Baptist church for three years. During that time, he had successfully turned the church back to its original purpose: worship and praise. Jack meant a lot to a lot of different people, but to Dan, he was more than just a preacher, he was a friend. When Dan was struggling with his spiritual identity, Jack was right there walking him through and giving him the encouragement he needed.

As with all pastors, there comes a time in their ministry when the Lord moves them on to a place where they are needed most. These are difficult but not impossible times to live through. Jack was going through that time right now. His work at the little church was so impressive, it had caught the attention of larger churches that were in desperate need of such a man. One of these churches had been hounding Jack for weeks, convinced he was the man the Lord had in mind for their congregation. They were very persistent and very persuasive. Jack decide to pray a little more seriously about it, and the Lord took over from there.

Dan first heard about Jack's leaving from a friend at church.

"Dan, this is Frank. Are you going to the service tonight?"

"Well, I thought I might just stay home tonight and take it easy. I've been nursing this cold and think it's decided to stay for sure. Why?"

"Are you sitting down?"

Dan paused. When someone asked you if you are sitting down, it usually meant that something bad was about to happen. He cleared his throat nervously. "Why?"

"Jack has been called to another church. He's making the announcement during the service tonight. Just thought you'd like to know." Silence jumped out across the phone line and screamed into Frank's ear.

"Hey, man ..." Frank finally said. "I understand. I couldn't say anything at first either. I know how much Jack means to you. I'll talk to you later."

Dan hung up the phone and stared at the wall. Anger, fear, hate, and a hundred other emotions flooded him all at once. He couldn't believe it! How could Jack do this to him? Was this the will of the great and powerful God Jack had led him to believe in? Get him all charged up and secure in an empty, meaningless faith and then pull the plug? He picked up the phone and threw it across the room. Now there he was, waiting to confront Jack, hoping in some way to change his mind and make him stay.

Jack seemed cautious on the phone when Dan called him. He wouldn't go into any detail, preferring to hash it out face to face. Dan could see his whole life crumbling before his eyes. It was always the same. You get close to someone and the next thing you know, they're gone! That's the way it had happened with his parents, who died when he was ten, leaving him to be raised in the foster care system of the state. Then there was his wife and son, killed by a drunk driver. Everyone he ever cared about was gone. Now Jack.

The rain showed no signs of letting up. Dan sat in his car, waiting for everyone to leave. He couldn't even make himself go to the service and hear the announcement. He sat in the dark, his emotions running through him, burning deeper wounds into his already scarred heart. With the news of Jack's leaving, Dan drifted back into an old habit. He stopped by the local market and picked up a six-pack. He was on his 6th beer when the last car left the parking lot. Waiting until its taillights disappeared into the dark of the storm, he reached into the glove compartment and pulled out a picture of his wife, Anne, and his son, Trevor. The tears were hard to hold back, but he bit his lip, placed the picture into his pocket, and reached back into the glove compartment, pulling out a gun. This was going to be the last time anyone ever left him! This time, he was going to be the one who did the leaving. He was going to leave everyone and everything behind. The plan was simple: shoot Jack, therefore killing God, and then turn the gun on himself.

He took another drink, finishing the last beer, crushing the can and throwing it onto the back seat. "Showtime!" he said, opening the door and heading toward the building. The rain turned into steam as it hit him. With the gun safely tucked into the waistband of his pants, and the courage he had found after finishing the beer now swirling in his brain, he entered the building.

Jack's office door was partly open. Dan could hear Jack rustling through papers, opening and closing desk drawers. As he peeked through the door, Jack invited him in. He staggered slightly, walking in, and Jack could smell the odor of beer on his breath.

"Come in, Dan. Good to see you! Just trying to get a few things packed. Great weather!" Jack knew Dan wasn't here for light conversation about the weather, so he went straight to the point. "Dan, sit down, you look rough. Can I get you some coffee?"

Dan's eyes, red from both the beer and crying, stared intently at Jack.

"Dan," Jack said calmly," I know this is sudden. I know you have questions, and I will answer the best I can, but it's like I told the congregation tonight, bottom line ... this is God's will."

"God's will? God's will? How can your leaving like this be God's will? What am I supposed to do? I can't make it out there without you ... I'm not that strong!" It all blurted out at once, as if the little Dutch boy had pulled his finger from the dike and let a sea of pent up frustrations, fears, and anger flood the office. He slumped against the doorway, grabbing his head. Whispers filled his ears: "He's a liar! He doesn't care ... he never did ... you know what you have to do! *Do it! Do it now!*"

Dan shook his head and looked up. When he saw Jack standing behind the desk, behind the boxes of books and papers, his hand reached for the gun. He pulled it out of his waistband and pointed it at Jack, hammer cocked, finger on the trigger.

"Whoa ... slow down, boy! Let's take things one at a time. Dan, I know this is not easy for you to take, but this is something I have to do. God has decided that there is another place that needs me more."

"Shut *up*! You're just like all the rest! Oh, sure, you say you love me, you say you care, but that's all a lie! This is the real truth!" He menacingly waived the gun around in the air. . "For once, I am going to decide who leaves who. For once I am going to do the leaving!"

Dan pointed the gun at Jack. Jack had never been in this kind of situation, alone in his office with an angry man waving a gun around. He looked at Dan. He could tell he had been drinking. "Help me God," he whispered.

"God? God? Where is God? If he cared so much about you, about me, he wouldn't let you leave. Everyone is leaving me! Well for once—" Dan pointed the gun at Jack. "—for once I'm gonna do the leaving. I'm gonna leave you, my home, my work, my friends, hell, I'm gonna leave God. This is the last time anyone or anything leaves me!"

"God cares very much what happens to you, Dan. That's why he led you here, so you could learn how much he cares and how much he wants to help you grow to know him more every day."

"Then why is he sending you away? Huh? Why is he so bent on destroying all the work he has done?"

Jack could see the fear in Dan's eyes and knew it was a cry for help. It was as if he had forgotten everything Jack had tried to teach him. "Dan, stop a minute. I hear what you're saying. Remember what we talked about? How God would never let us go through anything we couldn't handle? How we could reach out to him in our fear and pain and he would be right there to see us through the rough spots? God is not abandoning you, Dan. He is still going to be here. You don't need me to hold your hand. You have a faith that is strong enough to face the worst of life's storms. When you came to me you had no knowledge of God or his plan for your life!" Jack smiled reassuringly. "You were hungry to learn, though. Do you remember that?"

Dan was quiet for a minute and then answered softly, "Yes, I remember."

"That was God's spirit working in you, letting you know he has a plan for your life. The fears you feel now are not from God. God would never undo what he has begun. The enemy is the one who is making you doubt this relationship's validity. He doesn't want you to be strong in your faith in God. He's whispering in your ear right now, making you think you are not ready. He wants you to fail, whereas God wants you to succeed and continue to grow in his love."

All this time, Dan had been staring at the wall, clenching his teeth, trying to make sense of everything swirling around in his head. Tears were trying to come but he fought them back. His throat felt like there was a huge rock stuck in it and the air got real thick.

"Dan, part of being a preacher is knowing, listening for, and hearing God speak his will, not only for myself but for the congregation as well."

"Who am I supposed to talk to when I get into a jam? Don't you see what this will do to me? How can you be so insensitive?"

"Hold it! Dan, you and I have been friends for three, going on four years now. I have seen you come up from a broken spirit to a man of strong faith in God. Never have I nor never will I be insensitive to your needs! What you need to realize is that during all this time we have spent together, I am not the one who was making changes in you. God did that. He has done all the work. I have just been there to … well, point you in his direction. I am a preacher, yes, but I am also a man. This hasn't been easy for me, you know. I have been through hell and back with this decision! My family has been turned upside down and inside out trying to figure out what is going to happen. The beauty of it all is that in the end, I turned my problems over to God and put the burden on his shoulders. If I tried to rely on myself for the answer to this situation, I'd go crazy! Dan, God works the same for everyone. Only he can help you come through the rough spots. The trick is to let go and let him do it. He won't if we won't! Do you understand?"

The whispering was getting louder in Dan's head: *Do it, kill the liar and end your pain …*

"Shut up!" Dan screamed, covering his ears. Jack stepped from around his desk and took a couple of steps toward Dan.

"No!" Dan exclaimed, once again pointing the gun at Jack. "You stay right there!" The tears Dan had been fighting back finally broke through and streamed down his face.

Jack continued to pray under his breath. He kept his eyes on Dan, on the gun. All the while in his heart he was asking God not only for help for himself, but for God to remind Dan of just how much he was loved, how much God cared about him. Dan began pacing like a caged animal.

"Come, Holy Spirit …" Jack began to sing under his breath. He couldn't carry a tune in a bucket, but he needed an atmosphere of peace to fall on his office. Dan started to say something when a strange cloud filled the room. At first Jack thought it was smoke from a fire, but there was a faint sweet floral fragrance and a sudden calmness not only on him but in the entire office.

"Dan, I am here," a disembodied voice said.

"Who … who is this? Is this some kind of joke?" Dan asked.

"This is no joke. Why are you doing this to me?"

"This isn't funny, Jack. Stop it right now! Make it stop or I'll shoot! I swear, I'll shoot!" Dan screamed as the smoke swirled thickly around him.

Jack didn't respond to Dan's threat. He fell to his knees, bowed his head, and continued to pray. He knew what was happening.

"Dan, I am not leaving you. I am always going to be with you. I was with you when you went to the market and bought the beer. I was with you while you sat in your car in the rain waiting for everyone to leave. I was there when you put your family's picture in your pocket before you came in, and I was with you when you got the gun out of the glove compartment."

Dan was confused. Whoever this was, he knew Dan had been drinking, knew he had the picture, and knew he had the gun. He knew Dan's name. "Who is this?" Dan asked. "I have a gun, and I'm not afraid to use it! Come out!" As he said this he fired a round into the ceiling. The blast from the gun was deafening. Jack jumped as the gun went off, but he continued to pray. Whatever was going to happen, he was going to pray his way out of this situation, or pray his way into heaven. Either way, he knew God would take care of him. By now the cloud had completely engulfed Dan. It began to glow with a bright yet peaceful white light.

With the gun pointing toward where he thought Jack was, Dan squinted as the glowing cloud got brighter.

"Dan, let go … let me take care of you … let me show you how much I care."

"Who are you ?" he screamed again, waving the gun madly now.

"I AM!" the voice responded. Through the mist of the cloud a figure came toward Dan. He fired again directly into the figure. Nothing. The figure continued toward Dan. As Dan prepared to fire a second shot, the figure reached out and placed his hand over Dan's hand that was holding the gun. A warm peaceful feeling came over Dan. His arm went limp by his side, and the gun slipped from his hand onto the floor. The figure leaned in toward Dan's face. At first it appeared to be just a smooth surface that seemed to swirl like a blazing ball of gas, but there was no flame, no smoke. Dan looked deep, at first seeing his reflection, but then it changed. He saw the image of his wife, and then his child, and then his mom and dad. The images changed in rapid sequence, as if trying to find an image

Dan could relate to. In the blink of an eye and a myriad of images later, there appeared the image of a man Dan had never seen before but felt he had known forever. There was a kindness and a peaceful calmness in his eyes. It was as if to say everything was going to be all right. The figure placed his hand on Dan's chest. Dan felt himself being lifted off the floor and being pushed back against the wall. Normally he would have been screaming, kicking, fighting his way out of the grip of the man, but the perfect peace that was flowing into him overwhelmed and comforted him at the same time.

Jack tried to see what was happening. He couldn't lift his head. The presence of what he now sensed was the presence of the Lord was so heavy he felt pressed into the floor. Dan looked down as the man reached into him. He felt a tugging and then a yanking. It was as if something had attached itself to Dan and this man was trying to take it out. There was no pain, no fear, nothing but peace, calm. Dan watched as the man's hand withdrew, grasping a dark, wormlike creature that emitted an unholy high-pitched squeal as it entered the light. It fell to the floor, writhing in agony before evaporating. Again the man reached in and pulled more wormlike creatures out, and they all screamed that unholy squeal before evaporating into thin air.

When it was over, fifteen wormlike creatures had been removed from Dan. By now he was laid out on the floor, feeling a warm glow from the presence of the man who was kneeling over him.

"I will never forsake or leave you, Dan. I am with you always. Rest in me, draw near to me, and I will draw near to you," the man said as he stood up. He walked over to where Jack was, knelt beside him, and placed his hands on Jack's head. The last thing Dan remembered seeing was the man leaning over Jack and whispering something into his ear. He then stood up, the cloud of smoke swirled around him and he vanished. Not a sound, not a speck of dust out of place in the room. It was as if he was never there.

Dan and Jack sat up. Dan felt hung over, though not like he had been drinking but a different kind of stupor. He looked over at Jack, who seemed a little out of it.

"What just happened? Did I just imagine that or what …? Jack … am I going crazy?"

"No, Dan, we have both had an encounter with the Holy Spirit. Nothing could be more real than that. I wish more people could experience that. Not for the same reasons we did … what were you going to do with a gun? Never mind, whatever it was, I have forgiven and forgotten. We shared something special tonight. Something I know will change my life forever! Do you understand what just happened?"

"I guess I understand, Jack. That was Jesus. I mean, what I've always thought he looked like. What were those things he pulled out of me?"

"To be honest, Dan, I couldn't tell you anything about what happened other than we were both in the presence of the Holy Spirit. I was out. I didn't see what happened. I just felt this perfect peace. Then I felt hands on me and heard a whisper. Whatever you experienced … well, that was for you." Dan tried to describe the incident to Jack. He told him about the worm things and the face changes that occurred … but in the end, he too knew that what one experiences with the Holy Spirit is as individual and unique as a snowflake, no two alike.

"I owe you an apology, Jack. It's just that, well, I've never had a friend like you and it's hard to let go of you. I don't know what I was thinking. I guess I panicked. It's just not going to be the same without you here! I guess you're gonna call the police, and I don't blame you."

"Dan, there will be no police. I understand more than you think. Besides, I may not be here, but you know I am as close as a phone call away. I have this great phone plan, you can call me twenty-four hours a day! I pay extra for that. You can call and say 'Jack, this is Dan …' and then scream. I'll know what to do. It's a beautiful thing.

"I will always be your friend. Distance cannot change that and after what we have experienced here tonight, we are forever bound together. You know, Dan, whether you realize it or not, you have been as helpful to me as I have to you. You have a keen insight that at times has shown me a few things I didn't realize. In my heart, I know God has great things in store for you. That's part of what he told me. Don't give up on him after all these years!"

Jack walked around his desk and over to where Dan was sitting. He stood there, his arms stretched out, and Dan got up and embraced his friend. They stood there holding each other as the Holy Spirit surrounded them. Dan wiped his nose on his sleeve and sniffed back the tears. At last, all the doubts and fears were gone. He realized what Jack was saying was true. You have to let go and let God take control. They both walked toward the door, smiling and crying at the same time.

"Dan, this is not goodbye. I'm still gonna be here for a few more days trying to get things sorted out for my replacement. I want you to make an effort to be as open with him when he comes as you have been with me. I know God will send someone who will be just as effective as I have. Even more so!"

Jack was around for a couple of weeks after their meeting. The last Sunday he was there was an emotional one. He spoke to the congregation on following through with God's work, telling them that if they really loved him as a pastor, they would make sure everything they had accomplished together would continue. Otherwise it would all be in vain and he was not as effective a pastor as he or they thought he was.

At the end of the service, Dan came forward and volunteered for the pulpit committee. If the church was going to need a new pastor, he wanted to make sure they found the right one. Jack hugged him and whispered in his ear, "Remember, all this has been a test of faith. I think you just passed it!"

NOTES

NOTES

The Worshipper

The voice soared over the small congregation and landed on Jack's ears. It was crystalline in its perfection. Never had he heard such a voice coming from anywhere within his little church. He looked over at Stan, the worship leader. Stan was struggling to keep his little choir together. They had the "funk," that thing that happens sometimes— you know, that "I'm on the worship team today but tomorrow I'm gonna be a big star!" kind of thing that was so typical of everyone in Nashville, Tennessee.

Jack's little church didn't take up much space on the map as far as most churches go in Nashville, but it took up a big space in Gods heart. Jack was a worshipping pastor. He had spent years on the evangelistic circuit singing and preaching about God's desire for the true worshippers. God finally brought him and his family to Nashville, the self-proclaimed "Music City, USA," to start a church. So here he was, four years, two worship teams, and many many challenges later.

He struggled with his pastorate sometimes. There were demands placed on him as a leader that weren't placed on him when he had been an evangelist. When he was on the road, he could come in, do what God wanted to do through him, and then leave for the next place. The pastors at each church then had to deal with all the stuff that happens in churches. Now *he* was the pastor. Now evangelists would come through, do that *thing* God wanted to do through them, and then leave for the next place. Jack was now the one left behind to deal with the stuff that happens in churches. One of those things, in his case, was the worship team.

Over the past couple of years, God had changed Jack. God had grown weary of all the jealousy, offense, and pettiness that had begun to infect the people on the altar. He reached down from heaven and tweaked that little perfection knob in Jack's ears. It allowed him to hear beyond the talent that had migrated to his little church and hear what was coming from the hearts of the musicians. It was not a pleasant experience. While the congregation heard perfection in pitch and excellence in the execution and delivery of the emotional intent of the songs, between each note, each breath, each movement, Jack's ears heard a far deeper and more distressing sound.

"When am I gonna get my solo?"

"She's hogging that mike again! I wish the sound man would just once realize I should have the mike closer to me so that everyone could hear me!"

"Once Pastor hears my tape, he's gonna want to put me on staff immediately! He will probably want me to tour with him when he goes out again!"

On and on it would go, ringing in Jack's ears. He learned how to press through some of the most difficult situations in his life and worship, but this ... this ... how could God expect him to worship with all this static in his ears?

He looked at Stan as the last note of the song finished. There was almost a look of relief on his face. Jack knew Stan was dealing with the same thing. Not that he had been any great evangelistic leader, but Stan had the heart of a worshipper, and what he was feeling up on that altar was struggle, not worship.

The congregation, for the most part, was oblivious to all of this. Jack, with the worshipping heart that he had, had been able to step aside and let the Holy Spirit move into the hearts of people who desperately wanted to worship God but either didn't know how or had been wounded in spirit, pride, and flesh at other churches. God had taught them how to reach out to Him where they were and work through their wounds, pride, and flesh and seek the heart of worship. If only the worship team could do that. If only they could set aside their personal, petty agendas and open themselves up to the experience.

To come to that place within, where God-given talent surrenders completely to God's presence and the Holy Spirit flows through them like the living waters they sing about. How many of their lives would change? How many of their dreams would come true—or in that moment where willing soul meets loving God, how many lives would be transformed beyond their wildest imaginations? How powerful would the presence of God be for everyone who heard that moment be? It boggled Jack and Stan's minds sometimes to think of what each worship experience would be if they could get the funk off the worship team.

That was when Jack heard ... the voice. Jack looked at the faces of the congregation. For such a small church, there were a lot of members. Three packed services on the weekend made it difficult to remember every name and face, but Jack had learned little tricks on the road to put names with faces and was getting pretty good at recognizing the new regular faces from the visitors.

Stan was ready to turn the service over to Jack. Jack wanted to hear that sweet voice again. He stood up from his seat and walked over to the podium. The musicians had learned to keep playing softly, as Jack sometimes led them in another chorus from the song they had just finished or would start them on something new. It was a real pain to them. They loved the chance to play, but after twenty minutes, their minds were on their next gig, or getting home. Rarely did they want to stay for the whole service. There were some who would even slip offstage when their part was finished, abandoning the others while they made their way home or to the mall or wherever they felt was more important. Those who stayed, well, some did it out of obligation, and some really were worshippers and didn't mind serving, but for the most part, most didn't want to relinquish the spotlight.

"Welcome to the Still Waters Church ... where you can lay down your burdens and rest in the Lord! Close your eyes, lift your hands, and sing to the Lord your thanks ..."

Stan looked over at Jack, who gave him a nod and whispered a song title to him. Stan in turn whispered to the keyboardist, who started playing, and the other musicians fell into place. Jack turned his ear toward the congregation and asked God to show him the source of the voice. "Show me the worshipper, God, put a face on that voice!"

As the worship team sang and played and the congregation joined in, Jack listened with not only his physical ears but his spiritual ones. God reached down and tweaked a little knob inside Jack and filtered out everyone else's voice except the one he was searching for. It floated above everyone else, circling the church, and rising up to heaven. Jack looked out over the faces before him.

It was then that he saw the most remarkable thing … one after the other, angels stood beside, surrounded, and hovering over one woman. She was lit up brighter than any of the sanctuary lights could have shined on her. It was her voice that Jack heard. She was the one who was worshipping like Jack had never heard anyone in his little congregation worship before, or in a long while since he could remember. He looked over at Stan to see if he had seen her, but Stan was working through things and wasn't looking at Jack. He looked down at his wife, Sara, but she was pressing into the worship. Was he the only one who was hearing this angel? Could no one else see the angels surrounding her, bathing her in a holy light?

"No one else is seeing this, Jack. I am allowing you a glimpse of what can be accomplished in this church."

It was the Holy Spirit. He came to Jack anytime there was something Jack was asking in his heart, or when God sent him to direct, correct, inspect, and detect the defects that needed to be addressed. Jack knew him well. They had history.

"Old friend," Jack replied, "who is this woman and where has she been?"

"Her name is Sheila, and she was searching for a place to worship. I have led her here."

Then the Holy Spirit left Jack's ears and circled over to Sheila. Jack could feel his presence as it circled around the congregation, filling each member with a little of the special stuff that let people know He was here.

The tone of the service shifted as the Holy Spirit circled back around to Jack, flooding into him. Jack felt the surge and signaled

Stan to keep playing the chorus … coming back to the heart of worship.

Some of the musicians behind Jack rolled their eyes with an "oh no … it's gonna be one of those services" look. Jack felt it but knew God was taking over the service. There would be no sermon today. He fell to his knees and led the congregation in a powerful worship that lasted the whole service.

When the worship finished and the service was over, Sara came up and hugged her husband. "I knew in my heart this was gonna be one of those services! The Spirit was all over you! I'll go get the kids and meet you at the car."

She headed downstairs, thanking God for being at the service and for giving her husband the boost he needed. Like Jack, she too knew the struggles all too well. Her priority as a wife was to be sensitive to the man God had entrusted to watch over her heart. She knew from the beginning of the marriage that it was a package deal … you can't be a pastor's wife without accepting the fact that your husband was married not only to you but to the ministry. She had been through so much with Jack during his days as an evangelist that she was as much a part of the ministry as Jack was. She was his right hand. Her prayers beseeched God to unleash his power through Jack so hundreds of thousands of people all over the world would experience His touch through Jack's ministry.

Now, as a pastor's wife, it was even more difficult. Jack was a captive audience, more approachable. He had to be more available to people than he ever had to be before. Jack's choice to partner with her in starting this little church was nothing short of God's idea. God knew that through her Jack would stay grounded, focused, and empowered to do whatever God would ask of him because Sara was part of the package. God had so ordained this union for this very reason. No man alone could face the daunting task of facing all the demons a congregation would be carrying with them. It took a strong woman of faith to be a pastor's wife, and Sara was cut from that cloth. She had made countless sacrifices over the years, yet for every sacrifice, there was an overflow of blessing upon her, her marriage, and her family. Jack may have been the total package, a bag of chips and the dip, but she was the ribbon God used to tie and hold it all together.

As usual, a flood of people wanted to touch the pastor, talk with him, and cry on his shoulder. God had wisely instructed him to find leaders in the church to help bear the weight of this so he could be free to move where the Spirit led him. He felt a tug on his sleeve. He turned to see who it was.

"Pastor, my name is Sheila Warrens and I just wanted to thank you for being so open to the Holy Spirit. I haven't had a chance to worship like that for a long time. I really needed that, thank you!"

"No, Sheila, thank you! I could hear you singing all the way up front! You have such a beautiful voice. Are you from around here or are you just passing through? I would love to introduce you to our worship leader, Stan Johnson."

"No, no thank you … I am from around here, but I don't think it would be such a good idea to meet your worship leader … thank you …" She abruptly turned and disappeared into the sea of people vying for his attention. He tried to catch her, even tried to get one of the ushers to catch her before she made it to the parking lot, but it was too late. He wondered what he had said that had caused her to run off like that.

On the way home, he told Sara about the experience during and after the service. Sara was really good about reading between the lines and putting things into perspective, but this one had her stumped.

Jack was following a white car with blue trim. A woman was driving it. It entered the intersection just as the light turned yellow. A green truck sped into the intersection trying to make the light and clipped the rear of the white car, causing it to flip several times, throwing the driver out the window before landing on its side. Jack slammed on the brakes, instinctively reaching over to put his arm in front of his wife to protect her. He jumped out of his car and ran over to the woman lying in the street. Sara grabbed her cell phone and called 911 to report the accident. The green truck was nowhere to be seen. The driver had sped off before anyone could get the tag number. Sara went back to calm her children.

As Jack made it over to the woman, he began to pray. "Lord, don't let her die …" He was shocked when he saw the woman lying bleeding in the middle of the road was Sheila. The ambulance arrived, the police came, statements were taken, and Sheila, who had lost consciousness and had several cuts from the windshield, was rushed to the hospital. Jack and Sara made their way home, but for the rest of the day, they couldn't get the images of the accident out of their heads. They prayed, they sat silent, and they let God be God. It was the only thing they knew to do.

The next day Jack and Sara went to the hospital. Not remembering Sheila's last name, it made it difficult for them to locate her. Since they were not family, the staff was reluctant and legally unable to give out any information about a patient's whereabouts or condition. Jack started to walk away and head back to the elevator.

Sara stopped. "Miss, uh, nurse?" She called back to the woman at the desk. "My husband and I are pastors where this woman was attending church … we witnessed the accident. Is there any way you could just tell us if she was okay?"

Jack stopped at the elevator and turned toward his wife. She was amazing. She could be so clear when he was so emotional. It gave him balance. He constantly was thanking God for her. He had prayed for so many years for not just a wife but a friend, a partner, someone with whom at the end of the day he could be himself. He was a transparent man with everyone he met. There were no masks, no games, no hidden agendas, but God had searched his heart and found a rib He could use to make the perfect companion for Jack. That's how Jack explained it to everyone who commented on the strength of their marriage. God searched Jack's heart to find exactly what he needed in a wife and found a rib right next to that heart and fashioned the perfect woman for him. There was no other explanation he would ever consider. He walked over to the nurse's station where Sara was waiting.

The nurse looked around to see if anybody was watching and then turned back to Jack and Sara. "You're that preacher over to that Still Waters Church, aren't you? I've heard about you. I been meaning to visit, but I have to work most Sundays. My sister, Pearlene, brought me a tape of one of your services when she visited it last Easter ... I just about wore that tape out.

"Now, I'm not supposed to be telling you this 'cause of HIPAA and all, but if you can't trust a man of God ... who can you trust? She's doing just fine. She's in room 2478B. At the elevator, turn left ... end of the hall."

"Thank you, Nurse—" Sara started to say.

"Jeaneanne. That's with three e's."

"Well Nurse Jeaneanne with three e's, thank you so much. Is there anything you need prayer for?" Jack replied graciously.

"Pastor, this is the least I can do. Pearlene and I haven't fought a lick since she visited your church. I guess it's my way of saying thanks." She smiled and turned to walk away.

"Nurse Jeaneanne, if you will call the church, ask for Marti. She's my secretary. Tell her that I said to put her on our mailing list. I'll make sure you get a CD of every service. I'll even pray for a schedule change so you can attend services on Sundays." Jack smiled, and taking Sara by the arm turned toward the elevators.

As they rounded the corner and headed toward the room, Sara stopped. "I really feel as if we should pray before we go in there."

In the twenty years Jack and Sara had been married, he learned to trust her discernment. They stopped right there and prayed.

"Lord, you know Sheila's heart. You know he wounds both physical and spiritual ... use us however you need, to meet this woman where she is and do whatever you want, to get her where you want her. Heal her, Lord. In Jesus's name ..."

Sara had prayed her heart, but she had also prayed Jack's heart. God had woven them together so tightly, so strongly, they were an extension of each other. Jack thanked God again for her and grabbed her hand and squeezed it three times. It was their signal ... three squeezes meant "I love you." It was their way of letting each other know when it wasn't possible or necessary to speak. It was fun to have a secret language of the heart no one else could hear. It was one of the little things they did to keep that gift of love fresh and exciting. It was a small thing, but it spoke volumes about how committed to each other and their marriage they really were.

As they entered Sheila's room, Jack stepped back. The light around her that he had seen at the church was there even brighter in the hospital, and more angels surrounded her. He blinked, and in a flash they were gone.

"Honey," Sara whispered, "you okay? Sheila is talking to you ..."

Jack shook his head for a minute, looked around the room, and then to Sheila. "Yes, yes, I am fine ... I just ... did you see ... never mind ... I'm sorry. Sheila, how are you?" He walked over to the side of the bed.

Sara looked at her husband, shook her head, smiled, and walked over beside him. She loved him ... goofy as he could be sometimes. She slipped her hand over his, weaving her fingers in with his.

"Pastor, I want to thank you and your wife so much. I don't know what I would have done. I could have died. I just could have died had you not arrived when you did!" Sheila was crying as she said this. "The doctors say it's a miracle I survived the impact at all. I wasn't wearing my seatbelt and should have died instantly. I just have a few cuts and bruises and a mild concussion. I should be able to go home tomorrow."

"Sheila, about yesterday, after the service ... I hope I didn't offend you," Jack said. "I just think you have a wonderful voice and ..."

Sheila interrupted him before he could finish. "Pastor, it is I who should be apologizing. It was nothing you said. It was rude of me to leave, but you don't know my story." She paused for a minute, waiting to give Jack and Sara a chance to reply, but the story she had to tell had been dammed up inside her for so long, and the service the day before had been so powerful that it burst out of her before even she knew what was happening.

"I came to Nashville six years ago to do some songwriting and session work as a vocalist. I left a home where I was loved. I had a family, a husband, and a life. I had to fulfill a dream. I was a soloist at my church. I sang every Sunday, both services, special programs, community theater, you name it, I did it!"

She paused for a minute; she blinked, and Sara reached out and took her hand as the tears slowly began to fall. "I knew in my heart I was supposed to come here. To sing, to write, but my husband wouldn't move. He said I should be satisfied with where we were, that God had put us there for a reason. We began to fight. I went to our church and spoke with my pastor, who referred me to our choir director. He seemed so understanding ... so caring ... one thing led to another and ... well, it was a mess. He was forced to resign, my husband divorced me ... and, well, with nothing left to lose, I came here. It hasn't been easy. In fact, it's been the hardest thing I have ever done. At first there seemed to be hope. People at different songwriters nights were encouraging, they liked my songs, my voice ... I even signed a song or two, but nothing happened. Promises were made and broken so many times. I became a ... not very nice person ... to be around.

"I was working my second job last week at the music store when I met this couple from your church. They had heard me singing to myself; its a habit I have, and I don't even know I'm doing it. Sometimes I just have to sing, I guess. Anyway, they introduced themselves as members of the Still Waters Church. Ray and Maddie. Yeah, that's their names. They said that once a month they meet at their home with musicians and creative type people to eat too much and share songs. Just to celebrate the gift of creativity. They invited me, gave me a card with the information on it, made their purchase, and left. I had not been to a church since I moved here. I was convinced that what had happened at my old church had ruined me to the point that it wouldn't do any good to go. Ray and Maddie seemed more interested in me being around other musicians who were going through what I was going through in this town than they were in trying to get me to go to their church. In fact, they never even brought up the church except to say that they went there. They just really seemed to want to get together with musicians ... have their own little writers night or whatever, and it was so real, so enticing ... that I wanted to find out what kind of church had those kind of people in it. So ... that brought me there yesterday."

Sheila paused.

Sara looked at her. "Ray and Maddie are connect group leaders at our church. They are sweet people, even though Ray's sense of humor can be a little overwhelming at times. I know them, and they really have a heart for the creative type of people who are wired just a little differently than most. Ray is a pretty good songwriter, but he's even better at gauging a person. He saw something in you. Something you thought had been lost."

Sheila's eyes began to tear up again as those words pierced the last remnant of hardness that had so desperately fought to cling to her heart. "You don't know how true that is. When I was in the service yesterday, I wanted to sing but didn't feel worthy. I heard God say to me so clearly that He missed my singing and wanted me to sing for Him. It welled up inside me and flowed out so freely. I couldn't have stopped it if I tried. When the worship continued and Pastor Jack didn't get up and preach, well, something broke inside and I felt as if I was transported right to the throne room of God. You know …?"

Jack's eyes blinked a couple of times as the spirit welled up inside him. He knew that feeling all too well. Many times in his own study he felt as if he was transported to that secret place where he could touch the face of God. "How can we serve you now, Sheila?" he asked. "What can we do? Can we call someone? Is there family you would like us to call? Friends?"

Sheila looked away for a moment. She had been fighting the flood of tears that were aching to come out. They had leaked a little, but she had been strong enough to hold them back until now. She looked at Jack and Sara and then looked away again. This time she was unable to control herself and the tears gushed out in deep, soul-wrenching sobs. After all these years of struggling to make something of herself in this coldhearted town, someone actually genuinely wanted to do something for her. No strings attached.

She tried to express herself, but the years of tears, loneliness, and bitterness that had been held back for so long rushed out of her, making it impossible for her to speak. She grabbed Jack and Sara's hands. Sara thought she was going to squeeze the feeling out of her fingers. Jack recognized that grip. It was the last-hope, end-of-the-rope grip desperate people have. It's where the last of your strength meets the last of your rope and you feel if you don't hold on hard enough, you will fall deeper and deeper into whatever hole you've dug for yourself. You hold on to the closest thing you can grab. The strength of your grip determines the strength of your will to survive. Some people just let go and fall into drugs, sex, drinking, or whatever they can find to numb the pain. Judging by the tingling in his hand, Jack was pretty confidant Sheila's will to survive was just fine.

"It's gonna be okay, Sheila. God knows your heart. He is a forgiving and caring God. He wants to restore the stolen years. Right now, right here, God wants to set you back on your path, the path He chose for you so many years ago when He introduced you to the world on the day of your birth. He has known your dream since before even your parents were born. He has never—Sheila, look at me …" Jack's eyes were focused deep within Sheila's heart. He could see every hurt, every disappointment, and every scar.

Sheila looked up through her tear-filled eyes. She looked at Sara, who nodded supportively, and then at Jack. She felt as if Jack was looking deep inside and seeing her desire to make things right with God.

"Sheila, we can make this happen right now. God is no respecter of people, places, or things. You know He is in this room with us right now."

Sheila looked away in shame.

"Sheila," Jack said intently. "Don't look away. Don't give in to the fear. Let's pray right now. You, me, Sara, and God; you don't have to say anything. I just sense that you know in your heart that God is calling on you to make up. Are you ready to do that, Sheila? The God of second chances is offering you a second chance, and He is asking you for a second chance to show you how much He loves you. He is asking for a second chance to show you the wonderful dreams He has for you and the person He dreams you to be. He wants to introduce you to that person right now. How about it, Sheila?"

Jack looked intently at Sheila and then at Sara. The silence was deafening. Sara looked at her husband. She knew in her heart that this was who the person God dreamed him to be. She squeezed his hand three times.

Sheila couldn't speak, but she nodded. She knew in her heart that she was ready to stop the running and turn around and jump into

God's arms. She managed to squeak out a little "Please ..." between sobs.

Jack and Sara bowed their heads. To this day, Jack can't remember what was prayed. He was transported to that place, that secret place where he could touch the face of God. Sara says the room got really bright, but it wasn't what she would call an earthly light, and then she too felt transported to that secret place. A nurse who came in to check on Sheila fell on her knees and began to worship in what she says was the purest presence of God she had ever felt in her life.

And then there was Sheila, bathing in God's glory, feeling a peace she thought was never to be hers again ... and she could see angels ... standing beside her, floating over her, and asking her to sing.

NOTES

NOTES

A Two-dollar Suit

"Transforma." Wallace Robert Grimmel struggled with the word. "Tran-transfor—"

"It says Transformation Revival!" the man hanging the signs said gruffly. "My God, man, look at yourself! Now get out of here. This isn't for the likes of you!"

Wallace Grimmel looked at the man with the signs and at the disgruntled look on his face. He was puzzled. He'd never seen anyone sweat so much from such little activity in all his days.

He shrugged and turned to his shopping cart. "Just you wait right here, mister. I got something for you … something I know you need!" The shopping cart was piled high with garbage bags full of treasures that Wallace collected on his daily treks around the city. A perfectly good tennis shoe, a magazine with Britney Spears on the cover, even an old cell phone someone had either lost or thrown out. It didn't work, but it didn't matter to Wallace. He had a cell phone … and that made him somebody!

"There it is! I knowed I had one somewhere." Wallace turned back to the sweaty man with the signs. In his dirt-caked hand was a filthy rag of a handkerchief that he had found rummaging for aluminum cans. It even had his initials on it, "WRG." Wasn't his though … he found it … a ladies' handkerchief. It was one of his prized possessions. Sometimes at night he would take it out, look at it, and try to imagine what the previous owner looked like and how she had used it.

The sweaty man, disgusted with the fact that Wallace was even daring to share the same space with him, got indignant. "What am I supposed to do with that rag? Wash my car?" The sweaty man turned back to his sign-hanging duties, ignoring Wallace completely.

Wallace tried again to offer the handkerchief to the stranger. "It's to wipe the sweat off your face! You can use it. You can use it on your arms too. You're drippin on your signs! Them costs a lot of money I bet! I would hate to see them get ruined before they all got hung up."

The sweaty man snapped around and cut his eyes at Wallace. "Do you think for one minute that I am going to let that filthy rag touch my face? You are not only dirty, smelly, and poorly dressed … you are crazy!" The sweaty man then turned, took up his posters, and waddled down the block.

Wallace watched him throw the signs in the trunk of his car, walk around to the door, and with sweaty hands fumble with the keys. The sweaty man turned the key, started his car, and with gears grinding, sped off.

Wallace shrugged as the man ran the stop sign, narrowly missing the police car that was pulling out of the Freezee Treet. The policeman didn't look too happy as he turned on his lights and siren, wiped milkshake off his shirt, cursed the driver, and pulled out in hot pursuit of the sweaty sign-hanging man. Wallace chuckled to himself and then turned his attention back to the sweat-stained sign that hung crookedly on the telephone pole.

Transformation Crusade This Week Only
Second Avenue Assembly every night 7:00 PM

Something else on the sign caught Wallace's eye.

Healing and Miracle Service Wednesday 7:00 PM

Wallace crinkled his nose, fighting back a sneeze. He managed to stifle it only to begin another coughing fit. He had been doing this for three or four weeks. He took the old handkerchief and held it to his mouth as another spasmodic cough began. He wiped the blood from his mouth and stuffed the handkerchief down in his pocket. The coughing was getting worse. Sometimes he couldn't catch his breath during those prolonged spells. The bleeding had gotten more frequent.... He rolled his eyes back to the sign and locked in on what had caught his eye earlier.

Healing and Miracle Service Wednesday 7:00 PM

As he turned and pushed his cart down the block, he thought hard. *Healing and miracle service.*

Those words pierced through the alcoholic haze that he seemed to walk in constantly. Something about those words, healing and miracle. He sure could use one right now.

As he walked, his eyes scanned the area in front of him. To some people passing by it would seem as if the weight and shame of the world kept him from looking up and forward.

That wasn't the case. Wallace had learned to survive these streets by finding things, things that people had either dropped accidentally or purposefully discarded. Bottles, aluminum cans, treasures that mean another drink or another meal or both, depending on how lucky he was.

People could be so careless with their things. Wallace spotted an empty can across the street. "The eyes of an eagle, Wallace!" he said to himself as he dodged cars and angry drivers. As he wheeled his cart across the street toward his prize, it seemed as if the drivers deliberately sped up. He didn't mind though. He always tipped his ball cap, bowing his matted gray head, and waved them by. *So much anger, so much stress*, he would think.

Wallace bent down to pick up the can when another coughing spell came upon him. He wheezed, gasped, and choked as he slumped over on his cart. His head grew light and things began to spin. He closed his eyes and reached into his pocket for the handkerchief. As dirty as it was, it was a comfort to him, a symbol of dignity as he covered his mouth and caught the bloody greenish sputum that ripped its way out of his lungs and exploded out of his mouth. Wallace shook off the dizziness. He had exactly twenty minutes to get over to the recycling center and turn in his haul for the day. They all knew him over there. They were amongst the few folks in this town who even acknowledged his existence. He had been coming to the center every day it was open for the past fifteen years to trade in what few cans he could find. He always smiled and made respectful conversation with Tom, the guy who ran the place. Tom always tipped the scales in Wallace's favor when the haul was light, always making sure Wallace walked away with enough to get some food for the night.

As Wallace stood up to head to the recycling center, he caught his reflection in the window of the building. Staring back at him was a shell. His gaunt face, covered in an interesting pattern of dirt and whiskers, stared back at him. Wallace had not looked at himself for, well, he couldn't remember the last time he had seen his face. Suffice it to say the man staring back at him was not what he remembered looking like. The eyes were hollow, empty, and glazed. He ran his hand across his face. The stubble of whiskers and dirt and time felt rough against his fingers. His fingers. He looked down at his hands. They were trembling. Wallace looked at the reflection again. The torn overcoat, the oversized pants with holes in the knees, the mis-buttoned shirt.... It was hard for him to comprehend for a moment that he was the same person. He closed his eyes and shook his head. When he opened them again, the man was still there staring back at him in the same disbelief. He wondered how he could have gotten this bad, but the years of drinking had eroded his memory to the point that he was doing good if he remembered to eat every day. As long as he was drinking he seemed to survive.

The center was about to close by the time Wallace arrived. Tom was waiting for him with a big smile. Tom had a warm spot in his heart for Wallace. Wallace didn't know why. Wallace was just a shell—a dirty, smelly, whiskey-soaked shell of a man—but there was something about him that touched Tom. He always added a little extra change to Wallace's earnings. Earnings ... that was it! Wallace scoured the streets of this town picking up trash, junk, and stuff as if it was his job. In fact, if he didn't, this town would sure be a mess. Tom figured that, in the last fifteen years, Wallace had single-handedly kept the streets of this little burg so clean that it was no wonder it had won several awards for being so environmentally sound. Whatever that meant.

"Wallace, how are you?" Tom called out to the old man gasping up the slope of the parking lot with his cart. He looked bad—worse than Tom had ever seen him. "Whatcha got for me today, Wallace?"

Wallace looked up at the friendly face that had called him. Tom was a good man with a good heart. Wallace had nothing but respect and admiration for the man who had come to call him friend over the years. Wallace was wearing a coat that Tom had given him six winters ago. It had been new then. It had kept Wallace warm on those cold winter nights under the overpass on the highway, or when the rain drenched him.

"I got a few cans, not much today," Wallace managed to gasp out.

"Wallace, I do believe you have once again surpassed the ability of the community to generate enough litter and trash to do you any good, but let's see what you've collected, and we'll see what we can do today." Tom smiled as he grabbed the thin garbage bag from Wallace's cart.

The bag was the same one Wallace had used for several years. He never threw anything away. Everything has a use or reuse. Tom remembered when he had wadded up the bag as if to throw it away. Wallace got upset with him and made it very plain that the bag was not some piece of trash to be tossed aside, useless and empty, but was a possession that had a purpose, and that it was his property. Tom remembered apologizing and offering to give him a new one. Wallace said, "I have one. I don't want another one; it wouldn't be the same. This one knows me … knows how to work with me. Why, it's almost broke in; it's almost a part of me. Now gimme back my bag!"

The scale showed one pound of cans … not much. That came out to about forty-three cents. Wallace hung his head in recognition of the fact of disappointment. *Forty-three cents. Can't do much with that,* he thought.

Tom saw the look on Wallace's face. He had come to know Wallace's ways and knew that despite the fact no one would give him the time of day, he still was a man of pride and wouldn't accept charity. He had to convince Wallace to take that old coat six years ago. He told him it would be a personal favor if Wallace would take it off his hands, since he had "lost" the receipt and couldn't take it back. Wallace only accepted it on the condition that he could work it off. Do something for it. Tom let him sweep the office.

"Wallace," Tom said, "someone left this old shirt, shoes, and socks in their bags of cans, and my dumpster's full. Could you toss them for me? Maybe you'll find a dumpster over by the grocery store that has room. I just hate to clutter up the place. Could you do that for me, buddy?"

Wallace knew what Tom was doing. After fifteen years, he knew Tom pretty well too. Nobody left shirts, shoes, and socks there. Tom either cleaned out his closet or bought them at the Goodwill store. It really didn't matter. What mattered was that Tom was showing him respect by not just giving them to him. Honoring his sense of dignity.

"Well, sir, I guess I can do that for you ... but tell me, is forty-three cents fair market value these days? I know this ain't a lot of aluminum, but a hardworking feller's got to eat. Know what I mean?"

Tom smiled. He reached into his pocket and pulled out a large wad of bills. He peeled off $5.00 and handed it to Wallace. "Here," Tom said. "Consider this labor and delivery for dumping my trash for me."

Again, with respect, Tom had seen through Wallace's pride and met his need. There were no questions, no "don't spend it on drinking" lectures, just respectfully treating him like an equal.

"Wallace, you be careful. It's supposed to rain tonight. You want to ... uh ... you need a place to stay for the night?"

"No, thank you. I got a place. I'll be fine. God bless you for askin' though! God bless you for askin'! I better be on my way. I got stuff ... you know?" His voice trailed off and another coughing fit started to seize his lungs. He pushed his cart off the lot of the recycling center and headed towards Muzzy's.

Muzzy's. A small, dirty, overpriced convenience store. With the money Tom had given him, Wallace could get some smokes, a sandwich, and a bottle of Green Lizard Aftershave. It was the worst smelling aftershave he had ever smelled, but it had enough alcohol in it to chase off a cold rainy night. He might even have some money leftover for breakfast. Sometimes Muzzy would sell him one or two single cigarettes. Besides, Wallace only needed the cigarettes as a chaser for the foul-tasting aftershave. He parked his cart outside the store and went in to do his business. As he left the store, some kids were going through his stuff.

"Hey, git yer filthy paws off of my stuff or I'll—"

"Or you'll what?" the biggest kid asked. He wasn't really a kid. He was seventeen or eighteen years old, but looked thirty. The street has a way of doing that to a person. When you don't have and you want … you take. It's take or be taken. There were two types of people out here: predators and victims. What you were depended on just how badly you wanted. The guys circled Wallace.

"What's it gonna be, old man? You want some of this? Huh? I ain't goin' nowhere …"

Before Wallace could utter a sound, Muzzy burst out the door with a Louisville Slugger in one hand and a phone in the other. "You kids lookin' for some trouble? I got your trouble right here!" The kids scattered like roaches in the kitchen when the lights were turned on, but not before they turned Wallace's cart over.

"Wallace, you better get your stuff together and git out of here. I don't want no trouble around here; you get my drift?"

Muzzy was right. If Wallace hung around too long, those kids would be back, and he knew enough to know that he wanted no part of that. He gathered up his belongings and thanked Muzzy. Muzzy grunted at him and went back inside the store. The clouds started rolling in shortly after that. A light mist fell, and Wallace knew he better head to the overpass. He had holed up there for longer than he could remember. Most times it was okay. The concrete blocked the wind and there was a nice level spot right up in the corner just big enough for Wallace to curl up and sleep. His routine was always the same. First he would make sure no one or nothing had crawled up in his space. Then he would empty the cart and carry his treasures up to his shelter. He would then turn the cart on its side in the tall grass next to the overpass so no one would see it.

It was dark by the time Wallace made it to his shelter. The rain was starting to come down now. He stowed his cart and made his way up the slope of concrete. Settling in, he pulled out the sandwich he had purchased at Muzzy's. As always, he wiped his hands on his shirt and then proceeded to tear the sandwich into little pieces that would be easy on his gums. All but three of his teeth had rotted away or fallen out. This way he could eat. His gums were tender, and even soft bread hurt. He choked the sandwich down as best he could, coughing between bites. He reached over for the bottle of aftershave. At least it would ward off the chill of the rainy night and the tenderness of his gums. Each bitter swig of the liquid oozed into his brain, numbing it and him to the surroundings.

Just around two or three in the morning, the lightning and thunder started getting pretty heavy. Wallace was too busy dreaming to notice. He kept seeing the sign that the sweaty man had hung on the telephone pole. The words "Healing and Miracle Service" burned as bright as any neon sign he had ever seen. Then there was that sweet angelic voice calling him … "Wallace … Wallace …"

"Wallace, Wallace … hey … wake up, man … you were talking in your sleep. You got anything left in that bottle?" It was Fletch, the mooch. Fletch never had any of his own drink. He would just find someone who had and would mooch off them.

"Aw, Fletch …" Wallace said with disgust. "I was having a dream, and you mussed it up!"

"I mussed it up? It sounded more like I saved you! You was talking crazy in your sleep. Saying stuff like miracle healing! Man … you oughta be glad I came along when I did! Pass me that bottle. You don't need this anymore; you've had enough!"

Wallace looked at Fletch and then at the bottle. He knew Fletch was right. He had had enough! Enough with the drinking, enough with sleeping under the overpass, enough with …

The coughing started again, only this time it hurt. It hurt bad.

"Wallace, you don't sound so good. Maybe you should see a doc or sumpin!"

"No, no ..." Wallace choked out. "Just give me a minute; I'll be fine. Fine as kind!"

Fletch looked at Wallace. He was sweaty, yellow, and pasty-looking. He had the smell about him. Fletch recognized the smell. Shorty Bigsby had it just before he passed on! It was that death smell; like the insides had died and leaked out.

"Wallace, you beginning to get that same stink on ya that Shorty had! You fixin' to die. So, pass me that bottle, and let's drink a toast to remember Shorty by. Heh? Waddaya say, Wallace? Wallace? Hey ... you hear me?"

Wallace's eyes were glazed over. He was staring at something, but Fletch couldn't see it!

It was the most beautiful thing Wallace had ever seen. It was a man, a beautifully handsome man who shined with the purest white light. He was mouthing something, but Wallace couldn't make it out. He held up a sign. It said "Miracle Healing Service."

"Fletch, you see him? There, the guy in the light with the sign? He's ..." Wallace's voice trailed off. The man vanished just as quickly as he had appeared. Wallace looked around, but the man was nowhere to be seen.

"You're scaring me, Wallace! You're beginning to act just like Shorty did before he kicked off!" Fletch kept eying the bottle of Green Lizard laying over by Wallace. "You want I should take that off your hands? So you don't drink no more and see stuff that isn't there!"

Wallace knew better than to believe the mock concern Fletch was showing. He knew all he wanted was the bottle of aftershave and the cheap buzz it gave you. He looked down to the bottle and back at Fletch. He blinked, shook his head, and then stared back in disbelief. It was the man in the light again. He was pointing to the sign that said "Miracle and Healing Service." Wallace picked up the bottle and threw it over to Fletch.

Fletch could hardly get the top off to guzzle down the last of the nasty liquid that Wallace was sharing with him. He drained it and tossed it back to Wallace. "Thanks, buddy!" he said to Wallace. "I best be going! Got to get going … yep … stuff and things … I got stuff and things to do. I'll see you around! Lay off the sauce for a while!"

By dawn, Wallace was burning up with fever. He managed to get up and get his cart loaded back up. He started out on his rounds. By mid-afternoon he found himself over by the Second Avenue Assembly of God. That is where the miracle and healing service was going to be. He could hear the choir practicing. He walked down the side of the church. It was an older building. No air conditioning, so even on a rainy day there was no air circulation unless the windows were open. Wallace found a window on the side of the building next to where the choir was singing. He felt so tired. The wheezing in his lungs was getting worse. He was coughing up more blood, and the fever was raging. He found a spot beneath the window and just sat and listened. It was like angels singing.

"Amazing grace, how sweet the sound that saved a wretch like me," sang the choir. Wallace felt every word of that. He felt like a wretch; he felt lost, awful.

"Hey!" came a gruff, authoritative voice. "What's the idea sneaking around here? You some kind of pervert?"

"Well no, it's just that I thought, I mean … I was hoping for a chance at the miracle healing," Wallace said meekly.

"Get out of here, old man!" came the reply. "The only miracle you're gonna see is that I don't catch you and beat the living tar out of you for trespassing! Now get out of here before I call the police to come scrape you up and haul you away! Garbage! That's all you are, garbage! You get going or I'll …"

Wallace just stared in disbelief. It was the sweaty man who had hung the sign that had haunted Wallace's dreams the night before. Now this man was telling him that he wasn't welcome and that miracles can't happen for the likes of him. Maybe if Wallace sweated like the sweaty man did, maybe he could get a miracle then. He took a deep breath and held it. The sweaty man looked on in horror as Wallace's face turned beet red and then purple. It was no use though. Wallace was just too weak to sweat or protest. He grabbed on to his cart and started down the street. A coughing fit started again, and the sweaty man screamed, "Get that diseased stinking man out of here!"

That was when a couple of unfriendly looking young men came up behind Wallace and grabbed him and his cart and pushed them both toward the street.

"We don't let your kind 'round here! You stink up the place! Have a little self-respect and go clean yourself up!"

Wallace started to say something to the young man who was yelling at him, but he felt a warm wet sensation on his backside. He had soiled himself. It had happened to him before.

"Oh man! He just messed himself!" the biggest of the two young men screamed.

They threw him into the street, slammed the cart into his head, and made him see stars.

He lay in the street gasping for air as the three men—the two young guys and the short fat sweaty man—went back into the church.

The choir started singing "It is well with my soul."

Wallace picked himself up and grabbed the cart. He had hit the lowest point he had ever been in at that moment. He couldn't tell what stung most—getting hit in the head with his own cart or being thrown off church property. He couldn't understand how something as sweet as the music that was coming from the window could not affect the hearts of the guys who threw him out. He shook his head. The dizziness was coming back. He was soaked to the bone with sweat, and he smelled of his own waste. The fever was raging inside his body. He headed over to the recycling center. Maybe Tom could help him out. Give him a placebo, get him cleaned up … he couldn't remember the last time he had had a bath or a shower. Maybe if he cleaned up, got himself some decent clothes … maybe then heaven would let him into the miracle healing service.

Tom looked up and saw Wallace struggling up the street. He laid down his clipboard and walked over to him. He got there just in time to catch Wallace as he passed out in the street. Tom yelled to one of the guys in the center to come help him. They carried Wallace to the back of the building. There was a storage room with a cot in the corner. Tom got Wallace into the cot and sent for some water. He looked at his watch. He had promised his wife he would take the afternoon off and spend some time with her and their new baby.

"Wallace, you're a mess, buddy … we're gonna fix you up!" Tom gently undressed the old man. He sent one of the guys next door to the Goodwill store, told him to get some pants, shorts, shoes, and a shirt for Wallace. Tom stayed there and bathed his old friend. Wallace coughed and groaned. There was a lump on his head. Tom put some ice on it and continued washing who knows how many layers of dirt off Wallace. The stench was overwhelming. There was a couple of times Tom had to get out and breathe in some fresh air. Wallace finally woke up after a couple of hours. His head was pounding, but he felt something he hadn't felt in a long time. He felt clean.

"Hey, buddy, you doing better now?" It was Tom. "I cleaned you up best I could. You gave me quite a scare, passing out like you did." Wallace was still groggy but he sat up on the edge of the cot. "Where's muh clothes?"

"Don't worry. We had to burn your old clothes. They were a lost cause, but I sent Jon over to the Goodwill, and we got you some new clothes. I hope they fit, but if they don't, here's the receipt. You can take them back and get what you need."

Wallace couldn't believe his eyes. There stood Tom holding up a suit. It was a gold and turquoise plaid, and it was the most beautiful thing he had ever seen. He jumped off the cot and fell on Tom, thanking him, hugging him.

"Hey now, let's not get carried away. You put these on and get going. I can't let you stay here 'cause the owner wouldn't like that one bit!"

Wallace understood. He watched Tom as he stepped out of the room to give him a chance to get dressed. Wallace stroked the lapel of the suit. He looked around for a stool and saw the shoes and socks and shirt that Tom had given him the day before. They were laid out all neat and clean for him. Just like in a hotel. He slipped on the socks and the shirt. He looked at the ceiling. "I don't know you very well, sir … but I know you is up there, and I thank you for this." It was awkward, but it was a prayer. Wallace stepped out of the back room and headed to the front door of the recycling center.

"Well look at you! You look great! Wallace, if I didn't know you, I'd think you were a millionaire, a successful business tycoon. It looks good on you, son! Have a look at yourself!" Tom pointed to the bathroom. Wallace went in and turned on the light. There was a man staring back at him from the mirror, a man Wallace barely recognized. He was dressed in a loose fitting old suit, his face was clean, but there was an unhealthy yellowed pallor to his skin.

"Now, Wallace, me and the boys took up a little collection. It ain't much, but it should be enough to get you a decent meal and a room for the night. Please take it. It's all we can do, but we want to do it for you."

Wallace looked at the money in Tom's hand. "Why?" he asked. "Why you doing this for ol' Wallace? You don't owe me a thing."

"We're doing this because we want to, and it's the right thing to do. Now take it and git going before the guys change their mind and want their money back!" Tom said with a laugh.

Wallace took the money. He didn't count it, just shoved it in his pocket. It was a good feeling. Clean clothes, money in the pocket ... he had forgotten what that felt like. Tom handed him the receipt for the suit. Wallace looked at it.

One man's suit: $2.00

He put it in his pocket. Tom patted him on the back. "We got your cart out front. Everything's still there; you can check it."

Wallace looked deep into the eyes of his friend. Such kindness, such caring ... he had never experienced this in his life. He tried to speak his heart, but it bypassed his mouth and went straight to his eyes. Tom could see it shining, a sparkle that had been gone a long time from those old eyes. Tom nodded again to Wallace and watched him as he pushed his cart down the road.

Wallace heard the town clock chime six o'clock. He wondered what day it was. He wanted to go to the miracle healing service. He pushed his cart as quickly as he could toward the church. If he could get there on time, he knew he would get his miracle healing. He would be free of the cough, free of the fever, free of the pain.

The sound of angels filled his ears as he neared the church. A block away, he stashed his cart and belongings behind an old shed. He didn't want to be recognized by the sweaty man and his friends. They would just throw him out, and then he wouldn't get his miracle healing. He felt the dizziness come on him again. His head spun, the sidewalk spun, everything was spinning. He stumbled down the sidewalk pushing on toward the angelic sound. There was a flash of light. He looked up and saw the man in the white suit holding the sign:

Miracle Healing Service Tonight

Wallace smiled at the man. He seemed to beam a soft, bright, warm, friendly light that shined right through Wallace. A sudden urge of strength flowed into Wallace's body, and he made his way up the steps of the church.

The service was in full swing by the time Wallace found his way into the building and to the seat in the very back corner of the sanctuary. The spinning was getting better. He fought the urge to cough, pulling out his ragged dirty handkerchief and covering his mouth. Up on the platform, Wallace recognized the sweaty man. He was wearing a dark suit and tie. He was standing at some kind of pedestal. Wallace didn't know what it was, as this was his first time to be in any kind of church. Up on the front row were the two young men who had thrown him into the street. Wallace sunk down in his seat so they wouldn't see him. As he watched, he began to realize they wouldn't recognize anyone. They were jumping up and down, shouting gibberish he couldn't understand. The sweaty man was shouting gibberish too. Spit came flying out the corners of his mouth, foaming like a rabid dog.

As he looked around, Wallace noticed all the different people who were here. They were familiar to him. At one time or another, their paths had crossed Wallace's. Each time they had either ignored, chastised, or looked down on him with disdain and contempt. Now here they were all jumpin' and gibberish–talking, saying things like "*We love you, Jesus!*" and "*Praise you, Lord!*" It was a mystery to Wallace how they could be one way with him and be another way with some guy they had never met, never saw, or were even sure was real.

Wallace felt warm inside, like he was where he was supposed to be. He looked around some more and saw the man in the white suit sitting two people down from him, smiling at Wallace. The man leaned over as if to say something to Wallace, but vanished as soon as the sweaty man started talking.

"Brothers and sisters, we come here tonight to receive our miracle … our healing. In order to receive, you have to give. God's work costs money! Your sacrifice can help someone in need. When you sacrifice your needs for someone else's needs, God will meet yours!"

The choir and the band started in on another jumpy little song as people came up and put money in the buckets on the stage. Wallace saw what was happening. He felt the money burning in his pocket. He looked up at the buckets, and there was the man in the white suit, smiling, motioning for Wallace to come up. Grabbing the back of the seat in front of him, Wallace pulled himself up and headed down the aisle. The music was loud, like a party. People were jumping and dancing and patting Wallace on the back as he dropped all the money Tom had given him into the bucket.

Halfway back to his seat, the dizziness came on him again. It was all he could do to keep his balance until he made it back to his seat. He dropped heavily onto the bench and leaned over coughing. He felt a hand on his shoulder. He turned to see the man in the white suit. He was saying something, but Wallace couldn't make it out. He leaned forward again and held his head. "Lord," he said quietly, "I came here for a miracle and a healing. I am so tired. I know I have brought this on myself, but if you could just see it within yourself to forgive me and take this pain and cough away, well I know you will do it. That's why I'm here askin' …"

"Come with me, Wallace. The Lord has heard your prayer and has seen your sacrifice." Wallace turned to see the man in the white suit. For the first time Wallace could hear him. The man in the white suit held out his hand, and Wallace took it. They headed out the back of the church and out into the street. Wallace looked around, but no one noticed they were leaving. They were all too busy jumping and gibberishing to notice anything or anyone.

"Where we going, mister?" Wallace asked.

"It's time for you to have your miracle," came the reply.

Wallace took a deep breath and paused. He took another deep breath, and then another. There was no pain, no wheeze, no cough! He looked at the man in the white suit. He was just smiling at Wallace. "What do you think?" he asked.

Wallace stared at him in disbelief. He could breathe! No cough, no fatigue. He jumped and shouted, "Hallelujah!" He had received his miracle healing. The man in the white suit put his hand on Wallace's shoulder. A warm happy sensation flowed through Wallace.

"Wallace, I'd like you to meet someone. Someone who has been waiting to meet you for a long time!"

Wallace couldn't speak. He nodded approval, and they walked arm in arm down the street. A bright white light like he had seen shining from the man in the white suit surrounded them. Wallace stopped and turned to look at the small church. He could see that everyone had stopped their jumping and gibberish. They were all standing around someone sitting in the back corner ... right where he had been sitting ... it was him! He had received his miracle healing, all right! The Lord had sent a messenger to bring him home. He came into this world with nothing and he left the world with nothing ... nothing but his salvation.

Wallace smiled and turned back to face the man in the white suit. It was then that he realized it wasn't the fact that he had cleaned up and was wearing a two-dollar suit that had gotten God's attention; it was the fact that he let God clean up what was on the inside. That is what got him his salvation and his miracle.

"Is everything all right, Wallace?" the man in the white suit asked with a puzzled look on his face.

"All right? I'd say everything is pert near perfect!"

They kept walking ... vanishing ... into the light.

NOTES

Notes